WITNESS

BARE
WITNESS

KATHERINE GARBERA

BRAVA

KENSINGTON PUBLISHING CORP.
www.kensingtonbooks.com

BRAVA BOOKS are published by

Kensington Publishing Corp.
850 Third Avenue
New York, NY 10022

All Kensington titles, imprints, and distributed lines are available at special quantity discounts for bulk purchases for sales promotion, premiums, fund-raising, educational or institutional use.

Special book excerpts or customized printings can also be created to fit specific needs. For details, write or phone the office of the Kensington Special Sales Manager: Kensington Publishing Corp., 850 Third Avenue, New York, NY 10022. Attn. Special Sales Department. Phone: 1-800-221-2647.

Brava and the B logo are Reg. U.S. Pat. & TM Off.

ISBN-13: 978-0-7582-2233-6
ISBN-10: 0-7582-2233-5

First Kensington Trade Paperback Printing: October 2008

10 9 8 7 6 5 4 3 2 1

Printed in the United States of America

Chapter One

Justine O'Neill knew three things with absolute certainty. There was no such thing as fair play in this world. Men didn't love little girls, they abused them. And Sam Liberty, her boss, would never ask her to do a job unless he believed there was a reason for her to be there.

But at this moment, she was seriously pissed at Sam for taking this assignment. She worked for a man she'd never met or seen. She got instructions from him via a computer voice box, but she and her two counterparts *never* referred to themselves as "Angels."

For one thing, Justine thought she was no one's idea of an angel. She had a sealed juvenile record from when she'd killed her lecherous stepfather, Franklin Baron, and she fought like a street punk. It didn't matter that she was only five feet, two inches tall, and weighed barely one hundred pounds. There were few people on this earth that she couldn't best in a physical fight.

She'd learned early how to fight and punch, and she knew how to win. She'd do anything to win. Her days of being a victim had been over for more than twenty years.

"Are you going to mangle that bagel or eat it?" Charity Keone asked. Charity was a member of Justine's team and was probably the closest thing Justine had to a best friend, save for Anna Sterling, the other member of their team. The three women were closer than sisters and had been in real life-and-death situations, which had created a bond between them that nothing could break.

Justine had just done something that no one ever had: walked out of a conference call meeting with their boss, Sam. But the shock of knowing he'd taken a job with her stepfather's family's company had been too much. And she'd had to get out of the room before she exploded.

She should have gone to the workout room instead of the kitchen. But he'd rattled her. Sam, who'd been the one man she'd almost trusted, had rattled her. What was up with that?

"I'm not going to mangle a bagel," she muttered, tossing it on the tray in the kitchen area of the Liberty Investigations offices. She'd like to strangle someone—say, Sam Liberty.

Why would he take a job for her stepfather's family company—Baron Industries? Granted she didn't know any of the people in his family, and her name had been changed a long time ago. She scarcely remembered the scared girl who had been Jackie Conrad.

But still, she'd always avoided the rest of the Baron clan. She shook her head, trying to push back the past into that box where she kept it. That box she reserved for the people who thought wealth and privilege made up for a lack of morality.

Why would Sam assign her to work for the CEO of Baron Industries? Sam was the one person not involved in her criminal past who knew about it. Granted, the current CEO wasn't a Baron. But just the same, she didn't want to have anything to do with anyone associated with Baron Industries.

"Seriously, Justine, what's up?"

"Nothing. Just not looking forward to another cakewalk assignment. What's with Sam taking on all these CEOs? I want a dictator who needs assassinating, or a political prisoner who needs breaking out of prison."

Charity laughed. "CEOs aren't that bad. This kind of work is our bread and butter. Besides, you know that CEOs aren't necessarily easy assignments. We got beat up pretty badly protecting Daniel."

Of course, she'd think so. Charity was dating the last CEO they'd been assigned to protect. And the reason they'd gotten beaten up on Daniel's case was because Daniel had kept some key information to himself. A fact that had scarcely surprised Justine, since she knew that most men were usually hiding something.

"Whatever. I'm going to get my laptop."

"I'm here if you need to talk," Charity said.

"About?"

"Whatever's got you wound up."

"Nothing bothers me," she said, walking away and wishing those words were true. Instead, she recognized that feeling that had been dogging her lately. The feeling that her past was catching up with her, and that it was time to run again.

Bread-and-butter assignments be damned. She needed action; it was the only thing that soothed the restlessness inside her. Strategic planning and being a freaking bodyguard just didn't cut it.

She rubbed the back of her neck as she entered her private office. She had a window that looked out over the Mall area, and in the distance, she could see the Washington Memorial. She'd taken this job in what seemed like a lifetime ago to honor her deceased father, the tough old marine who had raised her to fight her own battles, and to love God and her country. She still missed him.

He was the one exception to her rule about men. The one that proved it. Her father had adored her and her sister Millie.

His way of showing them affection may have been considered unconventional, but Jackson Conrad had seen some real horrors done to women and children during his time in Vietnam. She knew that had affected him, and had been the driving force behind why he'd taught her and Millie to fight and stand up for themselves from the time they started walking.

She'd had her dad for only eight short years before he'd been killed in the line of duty, in some action that she didn't even know the name of. And then her life had changed when her mother remarried and brought them into Franklin Baron's home.

"Justine?"

"Hmm?" She glanced up to see Anna Sterling standing in her doorway. Anna was a very proper British lady who spoke with a crisp accent. At first glance, Anna seemed like she'd be a bit of a stick-in-the-mud, but she had a bawdy sense of humor that Justine always found refreshing, and a devious mind when it came to catching criminals.

"Sam wants you back on the conference call," Anna said.

"Sorry, I wanted to go over the details of this job one more time before the meeting."

"Sorry? You never apologize. Are you feeling alright?"

Justine flipped her off and grabbed her laptop.

Anna laughed as she led the way down the hall to the conference room.

The conference room was probably a little more high tech than most. There were three large leather chairs, each facing a large flat-screen video monitor at the end of the room. Anna took her seat on the left, and Charity was already seated to the far right. Justine always sat in the middle. The other women sat forward in their leather chairs to gaze at the flat-screen video monitor. "Karma Police" by Radiohead blared from the speakers of Anna's laptop. Anna's mood was easily gauged by the music she picked to play; Radiohead was a moody and melancholy Anna.

Justine glanced at her friend, wondering what was up, but Anna looked pointedly at her computer screen. Justine sat in her chair and plugged her laptop into the power supply at her work area.

There were no snacks or drinks on the sidebar. Conferences at Liberty Investigations were all about business, not about sugary foods or drinks. Which was entirely fine with her. Justine liked to keep her body in tiptop shape, since it was the one weapon she always had with her.

"Thanks for rejoining us," Sam said.

"Yeah, I'm back. Tell me more about the work we'll be doing?"

"I'm sending you all a file. The basics are that Baron Industries, an international pharmaceutical company, has constructed a new facility in the Amazon Basin that is being plagued by a local uprising against them. Their base operation manager can't handle it and just quit."

"Why are they building there if it's so hostile?" Justine asked, scanning the report as quickly as the information was showing up on her screen.

"The Peruvian government wants foreign investors there. It's the locals who aren't as happy. The Minister of Commerce and Foreign Trade gave Baron a huge kickback to develop there."

"Greedy bastards," Justine said under her breath.

"Why would the CEO go down there?" Anna asked, talking over Justine's comment.

"Apparently, no one else will go. His executives flat-out refused, and he is doing this to prove that it's safe for them and their families," Sam said.

"Is there a housing compound?" Charity asked.

"Yes. Nigel has already gotten a top-notch security team in place there, from Corsona Security."

"Well, at least he didn't cheap out on that," Justine said.

"He takes security seriously," Sam said. "Justine, you'll be pulling bodyguard duty on this one."

"Why? That's more Charity's specialty."

"Charity is needed to train the security force that will be taking over at the Baron Industries Peru facility. Would you rather do that?"

"Nah, I'm good with bodyguard duty," Justine said. She wasn't a good teacher. She knew one way to do things—her way. And if her students didn't pick up the lesson quickly, it just pissed her off.

"Charity?" Sam asked.

"That's fine with me. How many people are we talking about, and what kind of training?"

"The entire security team is close to twenty. But you will be training only an elite group of ten who will be responsible for securing the exterior of the facility."

"Why?" Charity asked.

"They have had a number of suspicious incidents at the facility—fires and vandalism. The teams you will train—and there will be two teams—will need to be able to identify the threat before more damage is done. They also need to learn to apprehend, and not kill, the perpetrators."

"Got it. Training here or in Peru?"

"Peru. Nigel is hiring all locals."

"Nigel?" Anna asked.

Justine's curiosity was piqued by what Sam had revealed of their mission.

"Nigel Carter, CEO of Baron Industries. He's the man that Justine will be guarding. Him and his nine-year-old daughter."

"A kid?"

"Yes," Sam said.

Justine was about to flat-out tell Sam off because they never protected kids. But Anna spoke up.

"Sam, we don't protect children."

"We do this time."

"I don't like it," Justine said. "Kids don't follow rules, especially wealthy kids."

"That's a stereotype," Charity said.

"You were a wealthy kid," Justine said bluntly. "Were you a rule follower?"

"No. But that doesn't mean the girl won't be."

"For Pete's sake," Justine said.

"Regardless, the girl is part of the mission," Sam said. "Anna, I'd like you on the computer security system. We need more than the passive system that is installed there."

"No problem, Sam," Anna said, her fingers moving over her keyboard even as she spoke. "When will we be leaving?"

"Justine is traveling with Carter and his daughter on the Baron jet this evening. You will meet them at the executive airport. Charity and Anna, I'd like you two to take our jet and head out as soon as possible. Secure the hangar that Baron uses in Peru."

"Will do. Is that all?" Charity asked.

"For now," Sam said.

They all gathered their laptops and notes, and headed for the door.

"Justine, I need a word with you alone," Sam said.

Charity and Anna filed out and there was silence now. Justine didn't sit back down because that restless feeling was back, and she knew if she sat down she wouldn't be able to sit still. So instead, she paced around the conference room until she realized what she was doing. That, and the fact that Sam was waiting for her to say something.

"What did you want, Sam?"

"To give you a chance to get it all out."

She shook her head. "You don't really want that."

"I do. I've known you for a long time. I know what I'm asking from you."

She shook her head. "I'm really pissed at you, Sam."

"I know."

"Baron? You know I can't work for them."

"No one knows who you are, and even if they did, no one mourned Franklin Baron's death."

She shook her head. "You're right. They didn't."

She couldn't tell Sam the real reason she hated Baron Industries. She refused to even dwell on that. "Whatever. That's all in the past."

"You have to let go of the past."

"I have," she said, knowing the words were only partially true. "I can't believe you gave me bodyguard duty with a kid."

There was silence for a minute, and she wondered if Sam was going to let her change the subject, but then she heard his low chuckle. "Yeah, I know. That was a nice bonus."

She gave the video camera, which allowed Sam to see her, the finger and turned to walk away.

"Justine?"

She glanced back over her shoulder. "This isn't about the past. They are just another client."

She nodded and walked out of the room, wishing like hell she could believe Sam. But a part of her knew that Baron was always going to be so much more than a job to her. They were tied to the man who'd betrayed her and torn apart her safe world. And a big part of her was always going to resent anyone who made money from them.

Nigel Carter didn't have time for meetings or for people who couldn't do a job without asking a million questions. He looked at Derrick Baron and fought the urge to punch the senior vice president; he had the feeling the board at Baron Industries would look poorly on him hitting the one Baron left in the executive offices.

And if Derrick was any indication of the leadership skills

that the collective Barons had, then it was no wonder they operated in name only when it came to the running of the company.

"You will be checking in with me every day, right?" Derrick asked for what had to be the fifth time since he'd entered the office ten minutes ago.

"Yes. I have it scheduled, and with the satellite phone, we'll be able to keep in touch. The Baron compound is fully functional. It's just security that's the issue there."

"I don't understand why Jenkins can't cover this," Derrick said, rubbing one hand over his thinning hair. The man was clearly nervous at the thought of being left in charge.

Because Jenkins's wife flat-out refused to allow her husband to go someplace where he might be killed. And Nigel had never in his entire corporate career been one who'd ask his people to do something he himself wouldn't do.

"I've already indicated I would. What are your concerns?"

Derrick rubbed his head one more time before thrusting his hands into his pants pockets. "My grandfather is adamant that . . ."

"That you live up to the Baron name?" Nigel asked.

"Yes."

"You're doing a fine job. Relax a little and things will go smoother."

"I can't screw this up."

"Why not?" Nigel asked. There was so much he didn't know about the Baron family, but to be honest, he felt like he knew the important stuff. Anything that applied to running the company was enough for him.

"My father was a huge disappointment, and was actually fired from the company. My branch of the family, well, Grandfather was ready to disown us all until I started working here."

And Derrick did a fine job in finance, where he was a highly trained accountant. But when he was asked to step outside of the world of numbers and into the executive management role for which he was also paid, he struggled.

"You and I will have our daily check-in," Nigel assured Derrick.

Derrick nodded.

Nigel clapped his hand on the other man's shoulder, showing him support. His earlier anger disappeared as he realized that what Derrick needed was someone who just believed in him, instead of constantly reminding him of the past, as Nigel was certain that Conrad Baron did whenever he talked to his grandson.

There was a knock on his door. "We good, Derrick?"

"Yes, thank you."

Nigel walked Derrick to the office door and opened it for him to leave. He looked distracted already as he walked down the hall. He almost walked into a small dark-haired woman who was standing in the doorway that led to the executive hallway right next to his vacant secretary's desk. She was vigilant in her stance, her eyes scanning the room. There was an aura of danger around her that was at odds with her fragile exterior.

"Can I help you?" he asked.

"I'm sorry to interrupt, Mr. Carter. I'm Justine O'Neill, from Liberty Investigations," she said, striding forward and offering her hand.

This was his bodyguard? He wasn't sure what he'd expected, but given the reputation of Liberty Investigations, he imagined he'd have a big hulking ex-football player, not this . . . damn, if she didn't remind him of the fairies Piper was constantly coloring and leaving in his briefcase.

But a warrior fairy, he thought, struggling not to grin at her.

He shook her hand, automatically lightening his normal handshake, but her grip was firm and hard. She pumped their hands up and down and started to draw away before he was ready to let her. He realized she'd had him at a disadvantage since she walked into the room. She was forceful and in charge—and clearly used to that.

And she was managing him.

He didn't let go of her hand and she didn't tug on it, but simply looked up at him. He saw the keen intelligence in her eyes, and the wisdom there as well. She knew he was holding on to make a point, and he thought she might be amused by his actions.

He dropped her hand. He wasn't here for her amusement. Nor was she here for his. He needed the very best in the business to protect his family, and he wouldn't settle for anything less.

"Let's go in my office and we can discuss your employment."

He hoped the reminder that she worked for him would put a dent in what he came to realize was her pride. She held herself stiff and tall. She was out of place in these executive offices, wearing a pair of black skintight jeans and a T-shirt that looked like it would fit his eight-year-old daughter.

Her midnight-black hair was cut close to her head and her features were fey. Bloody hell, he needed to stop thinking of her as some kind of sexy fairy sent to him for carnal pleasure. She was a bodyguard, and the last time he checked, sexual harassment was still illegal and frowned upon in the circles in which he ran.

"Yes, I'm interested in discussing this with you."

Her eyes were a bright electric blue and there was a steely intelligence in them. At once, Nigel felt a tingle of desire. Intelligence was such a turn-on for him, and he knew from that one look there was more to this woman than her exterior revealed.

He led the way back into his office. He was proud of the large corner office with the bank of windows on two sides. He'd worked hard to get where he was today, and had come a long way from the kid he'd been.

He never denied his past because it had shaped him into

who he was and he knew without that street-punk kid he'd been, he wouldn't be the executive he was today.

"Have a seat."

She perched on the edge of one of the big leather guest chairs that sat like sentinels in front of the large walnut desk he'd personally selected. Nigel propped one hip on the edge of his desk, instead of retreating behind it.

"I'm waiting for my daughter and her nanny to arrive, and then we can leave for the airport. Did Sam tell you Piper would be accompanying me?"

"Yes. And I'd like to ask you to reconsider. The Amazon Basin sounds like an exciting adventure at any age, but it is a very dangerous place."

"Ah, but that's why I hired you," Nigel said.

"Indeed. I know Sam has probably already explained this, but you are a very high-profile executive, and going into a dangerous situation like this is—

"*Idiotic.* That's the word Sam used. But as I told him, without this facility opening, we're not going to make our fourth-quarter revenues. And I'm not about to let that happen." But in the end, Nigel knew he had to go to Peru; there was no one else who could do what needed to be done.

His executives were scared since Paul Masters had been taken, beaten, and left for dead in the jungle. It was just the man's good fortune that he'd left on his satellite phone, so they could track his signal.

"There is a sufficiency in the world for man's need, but not for man's greed," Justine said.

The Mahatma Gandhi quote was one he'd heard many times before. He arched one eyebrow at her. If it were only greed, he'd agree with her, but he wasn't motivated by money. Winning was what drove him.

"Avarice, the spur of industry," he said, just to see if the intelligence in her eyes was equal to what he believed it to be.

He'd never been greedy, and if Baron Industries had been run by greed before he'd taken over, Nigel had made sure they weren't now.

"David Hume may have had a point, but that's hardly the case here."

Again he bit back a smile. He liked that she was smart. Yes, smart was a big turn-on for him. He liked pretty women as much as the next guy, but the women in his life needed to be able to talk to him as well.

"It's exactly the case," he said. "The Amazon Basin is a poverty-stricken area. Those people—

"Have existed for centuries without the help of Baron Industries," she said. "And that's why I think you should leave your daughter at home. There is a lot of danger inherent in the jungle. Bugs, plants, animals . . ."

"True enough, but that's neither here nor there. You are here as our bodyguard, and I'm going to trust you to keep Piper safe."

She crossed her arms over her T-shirt-clad chest, and he couldn't help but notice the way her petite arms framed her breasts. She cocked her head to one side and he knew better than to say she didn't look the part.

But to be honest, when he thought of bodyguard, he pictured Michael Clarke Duncan or maybe Arnold in his old Mr. Universe days.

"Will she—listen, can I be honest?"

He doubted this woman ever wasn't honest. "Sure."

"I don't deal well with kids. I don't have a lot of patience when it comes to repeating myself. So it's nothing against your kid, but will she listen to an order? I mean it, in a life-and-death situation there isn't time to be nice or try to appease someone's hurt feelings."

Any doubts that Nigel had about Justine disappeared; she had the heart of a lion. The kind of person he wanted guarding Piper. He suspected his daughter was going to take one look at Justine and become her shadow.

"Yes, she will."

"Okay, that's fine. What about the nanny? Do you trust her?"

"Why?"

"Because you are a target, Nigel. That means your daughter will be as well."

"I don't believe I gave you leave to call me Nigel," he said, mainly to see if she reacted. There was something about this woman with her bright eyes and petite warrior's body that made him want to push her until she did something. She was so buttoned-up, despite her casual clothing, that he wanted to see her react.

She rolled her eyes. "I'm going to be living in your back pocket. I think we should be able to address each other informally."

"I do, as well."

"Fine. Call me Justine," she said.

He nodded his head. "You may call me Nigel."

"I'm going to call you 'pain in the ass.'"

Nigel did laugh then. She was going to be a lot of fun to have around. He liked her and thought she'd be just right for the trip to the Amazon Basin. He didn't know if it was wise to bring her along since he was attracted to her, but he wasn't a lad of eighteen anymore, and he could control his lust.

Except when she tipped her head to the side as he continued to scrutinize her—he wondered if he was in control. Because there was something in her eyes as she stared at him, measuring the man he was, no doubt, that made him want to scoop her out of that chair and show her that he was man enough for her.

Chapter Two

Justine didn't trust any man aside from Sam. And even with him, it was an iffy proposition. So she didn't really believe Nigel could be the man he appeared to be. She paced his office while he was in a meeting with two other executives, preparing the men for his absence.

She totally understood that he had a business to run and that meant there were details to be taken care of, but she hated being brushed aside and treated like she was nothing more than a nuisance.

She'd been in contact with Anna and Charity, and they were already en route to Peru, and the capital city Lima, where Nigel would be arriving in the morning. They were in the same time zone in D.C. as in Lima. It was only distance that would take the time.

Piper's nanny, Constance Wareham, had been thoroughly vetted by Anna, and Justine was as confident as she could be that the woman was loyal to the girl. In fact, Constance had been with Piper Carter since the girl was two years old.

Justine didn't think that reflected well on the parents, but then who was she to criticize anyone on their parenting skills?

It was just that she'd always thought people who had kids should raise them.

Her BlackBerry vibrated, and she pulled the cell phone from her pocket and scanned the incoming message. Sam had more information on the group who'd kidnapped Paul Masters. Justine took a moment's pause as she read the report. This was the type of group her team was trained to go up against. She often wondered who exactly Sam worked for. The trio knew precious little about the man except that he paid well and on time. And he always had their back.

The group that had taken Masters were mercenaries with no real allegiance to the Amazon Basin or the people there. She opened the messenger function on her BlackBerry and pinged Anna.

<Anna>: What's up?
<Justine>: Any details on the merc team?
<Anna>: Not as yet. Should have something in a few minutes. I've got a contact in Central America.
<Justine>: Mercs change the dynamic.
<Anna>: We know. Charity is on with Sam.

Justine suspected that Charity probably felt the same way she did—the three of them should go after the mercenary team and keep Nigel and his daughter in the United States for the time being.

<Justine>: Ping me when you get an answer.
<Anna>: Will do.

Justine pocketed her BlackBerry and found that Nigel's meeting was wrapping up. The other men left and he stood and stretched.

She watched him, wondering what it was about this man

that fascinated her. She liked the low cadence of his voice. It was only her own rigid self-control that had kept her concentration on staying vigilant, and not on listening to him.

But he tempted her to think of something other than the job, and so few men ever had. Okay, no man really had.

"Is everything okay?"

"Why do you ask?"

"You're staring at me."

"Oh." She hadn't realized she'd been staring. "I'm trying to think of the right argument to use to convince you not to go."

"We already had that discussion. There isn't anything you can say."

"Nigel—

"I've made up my mind."

"And your word is law?" she asked.

"Of course not. I just know my own mind. And I'm not too worried about anything happening once we get to the Baron Industries compound."

"I would worry . . . that's where your manager was kidnapped."

"He was kidnapped in the local village," Nigel said, going around his desk.

"That is located adjacent to the Baron compound. Why was he there?"

"No special reason," Nigel said, glancing at his cell phone. "My daughter is downstairs in the limo. Let's go."

Justine waited while he gathered his briefcase, then followed him out of the office. She knew that Nigel wasn't telling her something about the manager's kidnapping. She pulled the BlackBerry out again and pinged Sam.

<Sam>: Yes?
<Justine>: I think there is more to Nigel going to Peru than to open a factory.

\<Sam>: Why?

\<Justine>: Gut instinct. And his manager was kidnapped in the village. Not at the offices.

\<Sam>: I know. What did he tell you?

\<Justine>: Nothing. He's hiding something.

\<Sam>: See if you can get him to talk. I'll have Anna do some digging.

Justine pocketed her BlackBerry as they got to the elevator. She scanned the hallway and realized she'd just been distracted when she should have been paying attention to their surroundings. She entered the elevator before Nigel and stood in front of him once they were both in the car.

"I don't think I'm going to be attacked in my own building."

"Someone really doesn't want you to open that factory, Nigel. Seems to me, getting to you here would make the most sense."

"You have a point. But access to this building is very tightly controlled."

"I know. I checked out your system before I came here."

"What else did you do?" he asked.

She glanced over her shoulder. "Read the mission specs and your background information."

"What did it say about me?"

"Usual stuff. That you graduated at the top of your class and have been on the fast track to the executive office."

"That's it?"

"It also mentioned your marriage and the death of your wife."

He closed his eyes and looked away. He didn't say anything else on the rest of the ride down, but Justine wondered if that was why he was reluctant to leave his daughter behind in the States. She recalled from the info sheet Sam had provided that

Nigel's wife Christine had been killed in a drunk-driving accident while he'd been on a business trip.

It was a crisp fall day as they stepped out of the office building, but Nigel's mind was stuck in the summer two years earlier, when he'd gotten the call that Christine had been in an accident. No one else had known they'd been talking about divorcing or that their marriage had been over. But he had.

He'd rushed to her side, arriving minutes after she passed away. Piper had been in the waiting area with Constance. That day had been one of the worst of his life. Wracked with guilt, he'd made a vow to himself that he'd never leave Piper alone. Never take the chance that something could happen to his daughter while he was gone.

Justine scanned the area while Marcus, his driver, opened the door to the back of the limo. Piper jumped out as Nigel approached and he braced himself for her. She launched her little body in the air and he caught her, hugging her close. She was talking a mile a minute about school and her day when she noticed Justine.

"Who is that lady?"

"Justine O'Neill. She works with me."

He set Piper on her feet and she slipped her hand in his. "Justine, this is my daughter Piper."

"Hello, Justine," Piper said.

"Hi, kid. Nigel, we need to get in the car."

Nigel nudged Piper toward the car and climbed in after his daughter. Justine got in the front seat with Marcus.

"Daddy?"

"Yes?"

"What does Justine do?"

"She's a bodyguard."

Piper nodded and then pulled out her sketch pad. His daughter spent a lot of time drawing and sketching. And Constance wasn't just her nanny, but also her teacher. Since Nigel refused to be separated from Piper, Constance had to be able to travel with him.

"Is there anything I need to know about?" he asked Constance.

"We're still on track with her schooling, and I shipped everything we'll need to continue her lessons to the Baron compound in Peru. I would like to arrange a trip into the jungle."

"That will have to wait for the time being."

"Yes, sir."

Nigel wished there were some way he could make this trip safer for Piper. Hiring a bodyguard . . . the best company in the business was all he could think of. He needed the plant open and operating, but he also needed to go down there to finish the job Paul Masters had been unable to complete.

He pulled out his laptop and sent two messages to his staff in Peru.

"Daddy?"

"Yes, Piper."

"What color eyes does Justine have?"

"Blue. Why?"

"She looks like a fairy," Piper said, nibbling on her lower lip as her pencil moved over the paper. He leaned over to glance at the drawing.

He shouldn't still be amazed at his daughter's talent for capturing people and landscapes on paper, but he always was. She was awesomely talented, this tiny daughter of his.

"Very good, Piper."

"I think her nose is wrong. May I open the partition and look at her?"

"Not now, Pip. She'll be on the plane with us and you can study her then." He wanted Justine to concentrate on her job—keeping Piper safe—and not be distracted by his daughter's sketching or questions.

Piper nodded. Nigel watched her make notes in the margin, the way she always did about colors.

He patted his jacket to make sure he had the papers he needed. He didn't like the way everything had unraveled with Paul Masters. He and Paul had worked together for years now, and Paul was his right-hand man. And the closest thing Nigel had to a best friend.

Now the man was in a hospital room in Lima, in a coma, because of this job. No job was worth a man's life, Nigel thought. Yet at the same time, he knew he was going to open that factory in the Amazon Basin, if for no other reason than because of what had been done to Paul.

Constance was talking quietly with Piper, and Nigel looked out the window, watching the D.C. scenery pass by. He liked the States, but there were times when he longed to be back home in the U.K.

But not today, he thought. He wouldn't have met Justine O'Neill if he'd been in Britain. And there was something about her that wouldn't leave him be.

He'd resisted the urge to kiss her earlier. Until his daughter was safely on the plane and all the details he'd had to take care of with his executives were handled, he couldn't allow himself to be distracted.

But she was there in the corner of his mind. He liked that smart mouth of hers. It was much softer than the words that left it would indicate, and he wanted to feel those full lush lips under his. He wanted to touch that curvy petite body of hers and find out just how tough Justine O'Neill really was.

Would she keep her guard up in a man's arms? Or would she soften against him? He had the feeling that once a man unlocked the passion inside Justine, things would get very hot, very fast.

"Nigel?"

He blinked, realizing the partition was down and Justine

was leaning through it to speak to him, her bangs falling forward.

"Yes?"

"We're at the airport and I'd like you all to stay in the car while I vet the plane."

"That's not necessary," Nigel said.

"It is to me. And you hired me to handle security . . ."

He nodded, distracted by the firmness in her voice and by how much that turned him on.

Justine went over the plane as she'd been trained to do. She learned her technique from Anna, who'd been trained by MI-5. She was a bit restless and edgy and wished she could say it was entirely due to the job. But that was only part of it.

The pilot was someone that had been working for Nigel for more than eight years. Anna had run a background check on the man, and they'd decided he was safe enough.

Justine ran down the stairs, back to the tarmac where Nigel's bulletproof Rolls sat, keeping the occupants safe from whatever threat might be waiting for them.

Justine thought about Nigel's little girl and it was painful to see her. The relationship between father and daughter was clearly a close one, and a part of Justine remembered her own father.

In her mind, her childhood had always been defined by Franklin Baron and the way he'd forced her to grow up. For the first time, she actually remembered her early childhood and the way her father had treated both her and her sister.

Marcus got out of the Rolls as Justine approached. She waited at the side of the car, sunglasses on to block the glare, and her Beretta held loosely in her right hand. She scanned the area around the tarmac and watched as Nigel hustled his daughter and her nanny toward the plane.

His vigilance told her two things. He was aware of the

threat to his family, and he took it seriously. She wondered what the hell he wasn't telling them.

She rubbed the back of her neck as she climbed the stairs and entered the plane. It was a luxury jet with thick carpeting on the floor and two desks set up on either side of the plane. There was a large leather couch on the right and four captain's chairs on the left. In the back was a bathroom with tub and shower, and a bedroom.

The walls in the bedroom had given Justine pause. The pictures on the wall were all very realistic and beautifully drawn. Yet they weren't works of art. They had been done on a simple sketchbook pad and then colored with pencils, chalk, or watercolors.

Justine secured the cabin door and then went up front to let the pilot know they were ready to go. He nodded and started the engines. When she returned to the main cabin, she took a seat on the long couch. Nigel, Piper, and her nanny all sat in the captain's chairs.

"Justine, this is Constance Wareham. Constance, this is Justine O'Neill," Nigel said. "Constance will apprise you of any changes to Piper's schedule."

"Very well. I'll need it the night before so I can make sure that anywhere you go is secure."

"I already do that for Mr. Carter."

Justine nodded. "I'll need your schedule as well, Constance."

"Of course. I really want your focus to be on Piper," Nigel said. "Once she's safe, you can shift your responsibility to guarding me."

Justine frowned at him, but said nothing as the plane taxied and took off. Once they reached their cruising altitude, Piper took off her seat belt and moved to the bench next to Justine. She had a backpack with her.

"Can I sketch you?"

"Why?"

She shrugged. "You have an interesting face."

"I do?"

"Yes, you do. I drew this from memory, but something isn't right about your features." Piper drew a leather-bound sketchbook from her backpack and handed it to Justine.

The drawing was a fair likeness of her. But Justine noticed that her eyes had a militant gleam that she herself rarely saw. She looked tough on the page, and Justine definitely liked that.

"So you like to draw?"

"Very much. My mother was a painter."

"You take after her, then," Justine said.

Piper shook her head. "I'm not as good as she was."

Justine leaned forward, but Piper frowned over at her. "Sit back the way you were."

Justine did as she was asked. "You will probably be as good as your mom one day."

Piper shrugged. "I'd rather be like Daddy. In charge of a large company."

"Drawing is just a hobby, then?"

"Yes, it is," Piper said. "What are your hobbies?"

Justine wasn't sure she had any hobbies. Her entire life was about staying focused, staying sharp, and keeping her body honed. "Kickboxing, I guess."

"Kickboxing? That sounds . . . interesting."

"It is interesting. It's a combo of a couple of different martial-arts disciplines, with a focus on kicking."

"I saw your gun before. Have you ever shot anyone?"

"Piper, enough questions," Nigel said from his desk.

She glanced over at him, but his attention was fixed to the laptop open on the computer desk in front of him.

"I don't mind answering this one. Yes, I have shot at people before. I'm prepared to shoot at anyone who threatens you, Piper, or your dad."

The little girl glanced at her and Justine noticed that Piper had sea-green eyes just like her father. "Good."

Justine nodded and bit back a smile. The little girl wanted her father safe. Piper finished sketching and Constance called her back to the bedroom for a nap.

"Will you sit for me again?" Piper asked.

"If there is time. I can't do it when I'm working."

"Thank you, Justine."

"You're welcome, Piper."

Piper walked toward the back of the plane and Nigel reached out to touch the top of her head as she walked past him. He didn't look up from the laptop where he was working.

"Your daughter isn't what I expected," Justine said when they were alone.

"She's one of a kind," Nigel said, with no small amount of affection and pride in his voice.

Justine felt that gap in her past opening again, reminding her of the relationship she'd had with her father. And she realized as she looked at Nigel that this man was truly different from the other men she'd met before.

She tried not to let it matter, but it was too late. She was looking at him differently. A part of her knew it had nothing to do with Nigel. Ever since the moment Sam had announced who the client was on this case, she'd been different.

She just hadn't realized how much of her past Nigel was going to be stirring up. Hearing the pride in his voice when he spoke of his daughter touched something inside her. That pride reached past the layers she used to insulate herself from caring about anyone, and pulled out the little girl who'd loved her daddy.

The little girl who'd thought that all men were like her own father. And she was just realizing that some men were. That Nigel Carter, despite his somewhat questionable decision to bring his daughter along with him to Peru, was one of those men who truly loved his daughter.

"Why are you looking at me like that?"

"Am I looking at you?" she asked, just to needle him. But she realized that she had been staring and trying to figure out how she was going to put him in his place—and keep him there.

Chapter Three

Nigel couldn't stop watching Justine as she moved around the cabin. She didn't stay in one spot, but paced like she had too much energy. She was a live wire, and though he already had too much on his plate with the business situation and his daughter's safety, a part of him was intrigued by Justine as a woman.

Intrigued, hell, he was in lust with her. It was her eyes. That fierce intelligence combined with her curvy petite body. He wanted her.

"What are you staring at?" she asked. Her voice was low-pitched and didn't carry beyond the two of them. She paused at the door to the cockpit, looking back at him.

"You."

"Don't."

"Why not?" he asked, having the feeling that not too many people questioned this woman. It was in her stance and her attitude. She acted like an Amazon and he suspected that made most people get out of her way. She carried herself like she was a tough-assed tank, but he saw past all that.

"I don't like it," she said, her voice tough as nails.

He couldn't help smiling at the way she said it. "So?"

"Nigel?"

He almost smiled at the sweet way she said his name, because he heard the steel underlying that dulcet tone. "Hmm?"

She came a few steps closer, stopping when less than three feet separated them. She put one hand on her hip and the other one hovered just over the butt of her handgun, which she'd holstered on her hip for all the world to see.

"I'm trained to kill. You know that, right?"

"Are you threatening me?" he asked, not feeling threatened in the least. He wondered what exactly it said about him that he was turned on by the strength inside her. A part of him acknowledged that with Justine, he'd never really have to worry about her ability to take care of herself.

"No, just making sure you have all the information necessary to keep yourself healthy."

He laughed. He couldn't help it. Because there was an element of teasing in what she'd said.

"I'm not just a CEO," he said.

She arched one eyebrow. "I didn't see a *Guns & Ammo* magazine subscription in your profile."

"You looked?"

"Yes."

"What did you see?"

"Three kids' magazines and a bunch of boring business journals."

"Boring?"

"Yes, boring . . . frankly, Nigel, I had expected something a bit more exciting."

He stood up from behind his desk, blocking her path as she turned to pace by him. She drew up short so their bodies didn't touch. But Nigel wanted to feel her against him.

He put one hand on her hip and she crossed her arms over her chest. All the animation and teasing that had been part of her just a minute earlier was gone now. Completely shut down as if a switch had been thrown.

"What's up?"

She shook her head.

He removed his hand from her waist and she shuddered. There was more here than met the eye. More to this than he was seeing, and for a quick affair—and that was really all he could have with a woman like Justine—he didn't need to plumb her psyche. He just needed to figure out if the lust he felt was one-sided.

But he wasn't a cad. Wasn't the kind of man who thought only of his own needs.

"Should I apologize?" he asked as she continued to stand there with her arms crossed over her chest.

She shook her head again.

"No. It's just . . . I don't like to be touched."

"Is it a bodyguard thing?"

"What?"

"You know, your instincts are honed to a trigger point."

She arched an eyebrow at him. "Are you making fun of me?"

"Never. I was trying . . . trying to tease a smile back on your lips."

"Why?"

"I like your smile."

"You do?"

"Yes."

"Why?"

He shook his head this time. "You mustn't get many compliments."

She shrugged. "Honestly, I don't trust them."

"Why not?"

"What's with you and all the questions?"

"I'm a CEO. I thrive on information."

"So do bodyguards," she said.

The teasing note was back in her voice, and he felt a little thrill of victory at having done that. "Why are you a bodyguard?"

"Well, to be honest, I'm usually more of a weapons expert and marksman. For most assignments we take on, Charity functions as the bodyguard."

"Why is that?"

"She's tall and gorgeous, just the sort of person that makes most assailants think they don't have a thing to worry about."

"And you're not."

She gestured to her short frame. "Height is one thing I've never needed."

"No?"

"No," she said. "I learned early on that if I don't quit, I can take anyone."

"Can you take me?"

"Easily," she said.

He took two steps toward her. The plane rocked and bucked, and all the playfulness she'd had a second ago disappeared as she used her body to take him down to the floor, and braced both of their bodies.

When the plane leveled itself, she knew it had to be turbulence and not an engine malfunction, or any other danger. But her heart was racing, and it had nothing at all to do with the security of Nigel Carter or his daughter.

Justine closed her eyes, but that just made everything... better. All of her other senses came to life. The feel of his hard body under hers, the scent of his spicy aftershave, the sound of each exhalation of his minty breath against her cheek.

She opened her eyes as Nigel's hands settled low on her waist. This time it wasn't different. His hand was in the exact same spot that had worried her when they'd been standing toe-to-toe. But now it didn't bother her. She was on top of him.

She shifted her weight, letting her legs slide off his hips so she was braced above him. He looked up, his green eyes watching her. His hold on her was loose and not threatening at all. She wanted to stay there.

His eyes slid lower, his gaze moving over her face and lingering on her lips. They felt dry and she licked them.

He moaned and leaned up, his own tongue tracing the same path hers had just taken. She let her own tongue touch his and he breathed into her mouth. The taste of him was delicious. He slid one of his hands up her back to her neck, cupping her head as his mouth took hers, his lips rubbing against hers as his tongue teased hers.

The touch was featherlight, and though she was the one in the position of power, he was totally in control in this moment, and a feeling she'd never experienced before swamped her.

Her breasts felt fuller as his mouth continued to move over hers. He caught her lower lip in his mouth, held it lightly between his teeth, and sucked on it. She moaned deep in her throat and shifted against him, wanting to feel him between her legs. She started to lower her hips before she realized what she was doing.

She jerked back, pushed herself to her feet, and offered Nigel her hand. He ignored it and stood up next to her. He towered over her, and she tried not to focus on the fact that he'd felt warm and had smelled good when she'd been lying on top of him.

She didn't get close to men. She just never did, but that one moment of body-to-body contact was setting off alarm bells in her body. And not the flight ones, for once. She'd wanted . . . ah, hell, she'd wanted to stay on top of him, continue kissing him until . . .

What the hell? She didn't think about sex. Ever. Especially not on the job.

She brushed her hands down her hips and turned away from Nigel. "I'm going to check with the pilot and make sure that was just normal turbulence."

"What else would it be?"

She had no idea; she only knew she needed to get away before she did something she couldn't control. Something that was not in her normal m.o.

Her heartbeat was racing, her blood flowing heavier in her veins, and her entire body was alive. Her skin was sensitive, as a strange restlessness moved through her. She knew it was arousal, but she'd never experienced it before. She wasn't a virgin, but she'd never really made love. Never experienced these feelings before, and like another new and unfamiliar feeling, it made her edgy.

"Something else," she said, trying to get her head around what had happened. Trying desperately to figure out how to calm her body. She felt jittery, and she knew herself well enough to know that she was going to do something stupid if she didn't get away from Nigel.

He gave her one of those cocky grins of his and she had the feeling that he knew exactly how being close to him affected her.

"It could be an engine out, or maybe a time-detonated bomb set to go off once we're in flight. Or maybe some kind of odorless gas release that will kill everyone on the flight."

He shuddered, and she felt mean as soon as she'd started talking. He turned on his heel and went back to check on Piper, no doubt. She hated that about herself. But she knew she couldn't change it.

She'd always been able to find someone's weak spot and manipulate it. The fact that she'd used his concern for his daughter's safety to make him feel the way she did, was . . . disgusting, she thought.

How could she cause him to worry about his child, just because he'd kissed her and she hadn't known how to handle it?

She cursed under her breath, feeling angry and sad as she moved to the cabin door that led to the cockpit. She hesitated there, not wanting to face the pilot until she was more sure of herself.

She took a deep breath, but yoga breathing never really worked for her. She needed to kick something or punch something. She needed a physical outlet for these emotions.

She stood there, her hands shaking. Goddammit, why were her hands shaking? Facing down an armed assailant didn't bother her, but being kissed by a man did. Damn, she was seriously screwed up, wasn't she?

She wanted off this assignment, she thought. For the first time since she'd left the juvenile detention center, she wanted to run. Was this just more of the same feeling she'd had when Sam had told her they were taking an assignment from Baron? Or was it something else?

Her gut said it had something to do with Nigel. Nigel Carter and his sexy eyes, teasing questions, and soft kisses. He'd held her loosely . . . over the years, she'd had men come on to her before, but never the way he had.

There had been no doubt he was in control, but he hadn't forced her, hadn't tried to take anything from her . . . he'd just coaxed her gently until she responded.

She laid her head forward on the cabin door, realizing that she had no idea how to handle Nigel Carter. She could protect him and his daughter from any outside threat, but she had absolutely no fucking idea how to handle the man when they were alone.

* * *

Nigel exited the bedroom at the back of the plane and froze. Justine stood where he'd left her, but her demeanor had totally changed. She seemed smaller; for the first time since he'd met her, he was really aware of her height. He didn't know what had shattered her Amazon persona, but he had a feeling it had to do with whatever had sparked her temper.

Hell, he knew he had sparked her temper. Knew she'd deliberately preyed on his fears about his daughter. He was angry at himself for the weakness. But it didn't take a rocket scientist to figure out that Piper was his weakness. Everyone at Baron knew it.

"Justine?"

She straightened up and when she turned, he saw a hint of vulnerability in her eyes. But it was gone in a flash and instead, he was staring into those hard-as-steel blue eyes of hers. The keen intelligence and the strength he'd first seen in her was back.

"Yes?"

"Everything okay with the pilot?" he asked, pulling back from his own need to get some kind of retribution from her for scaring him.

"I haven't checked yet. I'll be back in a second."

She opened the door to the cockpit and Nigel went to his desk. He sat down in the big leather chair he'd earned. He looked around the private jet and instead of seeing the hard work that had brought him here, he saw the safety it gave him and Piper. The luxury of flying when they wanted to, instead of having to comply with an airline's schedule.

He saw the opportunity that he'd been given by using his chutzpah and intelligence to climb his way to the top of the corporate ladder, and he knew there were men and women in the Amazon Basin who might want the same thing. Men and women in Peru and Brazil who would be happy for the opportunity to carve out their own niche in Baron Industries the way he had.

He had never questioned why he was determined to open the operation in Cusco. From the first time he'd met with the commerce officials, he'd understood what they wanted to do. The shared vision had been enough incentive, the financial ones simply a bonus.

The door opened, and Justine reentered the main cabin. Nigel glanced up from his laptop and their eyes met. She stood there with none of the restless energy that had been so markedly different from what he'd seen from her earlier.

"Everything okay?"

"Yes, the captain took us to a higher altitude to avoid any more turbulence. We will probably arrive in Lima a bit earlier than we had anticipated."

"That's fine."

She shrugged.

"Justine?"

"Yes?"

"I'm not sorry I kissed you."

She looked at him for the first time since she'd reentered the cabin, really looked at him, and he realized that he'd inadvertently hit the problem. She was nervous about that embrace. He knew then that a simple affair wasn't in the cards for the two of them.

He rubbed the back of his neck and waited. Finally, she walked forward and sat in the captain's chair in front of his desk.

"I'm not used to kissing my clients," she said at last, her voice low-pitched and the slightest bit husky.

"Good."

A slight smile lit her lips. "You aren't what I expected."

He arched one eyebrow. "What did you expect?"

"Some moneygrubbing, type-A-personality executive."

"Moneygrubbing?"

"Ya know what I mean. The locals don't want you in their area, but you are going anyway because of the money."

He noticed she'd changed the topic, turned the conversation toward business, and away from the personal. "You know nothing about why I'm determined to build that operation."

"You're right. That's what I was saying. At first, I thought you were just in it for the money, but now . . ."

"Now?"

"I'm not so sure."

"Good."

"You like saying that, don't you?"

"Yes, I do."

"Why?"

"I have the feeling not many men get the better of you, Justine."

"You didn't get the better of me," she said, her feisty spirit sparking again.

Nigel leaned forward on his desk, resting his elbows on the blotter. "I got the very best of you, Justine."

"How do you figure?"

Her spark and her spirit turned him on like nothing else could. Each new thing he learned about this woman showed him that she was as multifaceted as a diamond, and just as rare. There was so much more to Justine O'Neill than just bodyguard.

"By your own words. You don't kiss your clients, yet you did kiss me."

She shook her head and licked her lips. Those tempting lips that he'd kissed once and longed to have under his again.

"You are impossible."

But he'd heard that before. His tenacity often pissed off people in the business world, and though his board was happy with his results, he knew there were times when a lot of people wished he'd just back down.

"Not really. I just go after what I want."

She leaned forward, coming closer to him than she had since the moment their embrace had ended.

"You don't want me, Nigel."

"Let me be the judge of that."

She shook her head. "I'm not what you think I am."

"I think you're a virago."

Justine leaned forward on his desk. "That word has two meanings."

"I know. I don't use words if I'm unclear on what they mean."

"I don't find either offensive," she said.

Nigel wanted to laugh. Most women would be bothered by having it implied that she or her behavior was violent. But he'd meant that she was strong and brave. She might well be the bravest woman he knew.

And it wasn't just because she handled weapons with the same ease most women applied their lipstick. Or the fact that he knew that physically, she could and would defend him and his daughter. Or even the quick wit that showed him she was more than just a killer with a gun who'd been hired to do a job.

Her braveness came from the fact that he'd shaken her when he'd kissed her, and she was still sitting across from him. In his experience, most women didn't have staying power when faced with something that wasn't comfortable for them.

His own mother had left, rather than stay and raise a boy who'd grown taller than she was. She turned into a stranger, and as he looked at the pixie-featured bodyguard, he realized he wanted her as a woman because she wasn't one to run away.

Chapter Four

Justine spent the rest of the flight on the BlackBerry, communicating with Sam and the team and pretending that Nigel hadn't shaken everything she'd believed about herself and men. She knew it wasn't every man who could affect her this way. Just Nigel, and that was what bothered her. She didn't want him to be different from other men.

She wanted to continue distrusting him the way she did all men. Even Sam didn't get her total trust. But Nigel was different. And she couldn't help glancing over at him when she thought he wasn't watching.

"Do you like my dad?"

Justine glanced to the aisle where Piper was standing, watching her with those too-old eyes of hers. Justine shrugged. "My job is to protect you and your dad, not like you."

"Why are you watching him?"

"He's not like most men I've met."

Piper smiled. "He's better, right?"

Justine had to smile at the little girl. There was such pride in her voice and such . . . hero worship when she looked at her dad. Piper thought her father was Superman. And Justine was glad for that. Little girls should have daddies who were better than superheroes.

"You think?"

"Yes. And you do, too."

"I do?"

"Yes, you do."

Those wise eyes narrowed on her, and Justine wondered how a kid who wasn't even ten could have such insight into human nature.

"I don't think he's better or worse than any man," Justine said at last. "He's just different from what I'm used to."

"What's your daddy like?" Piper asked.

And Justine felt her heart lurch a bit. She never talked about Jackson Conrad or Millie. Never talked about her family. No one ever asked. She just lived her life and did her job, and that was the extent of it. She'd become this bit of nothingness that was simply her job.

"Justine?"

"Hmm?"

"Do you have a dad?"

"He died when I was eight."

"Oh. I'm sorry."

"Me, too. He wasn't anything like your dad, but he was the best dad for me."

Piper sat down in the seat across from Justine and tipped her head to the side, her concentration intent as she watched her. Those eyes that were so like Nigel's and yet so unique were studying her, but this time Justine knew that Piper had switched from the little girl to the artist. She had the same deep concentration that Justine had when she was working. She could shut off the real world and fall into a world where life was just about the target and the job.

She reached for her handgun, fingered the butt of her gun, and felt soothed by it, almost could smell the Old Spice aftershave her father used to wear. In her mind she heard his advice, the only thing he said to her and her sister every night.

"Vigilance is key."

Justine pushed to her feet as Piper got out a sketchbook and pencil. She paced the aisle, watching for dangers in a place where she knew there weren't any. But her father had instilled in her the need to always be on her guard. Something she'd forgotten only once. But then Franklin Baron had reminded her of it with his betrayal.

She walked by Nigel's work desk, pretending she didn't notice him or the spicy clean scent of his aftershave. On her return trip, his hand snaked out and clamped down on her wrist. She twisted her hand in his grip and reversed the hold so that he was her captive. He did the same thing, and she had the feeling they were well matched in this. Were they physical equals?

She doubted it. Even with her training in hand-to-hand combat and street fighting, he had brute strength on his side, and that could never be discounted.

She raised one eyebrow at him and tugged on her hand. He let her go immediately.

"I'd like a word with you," he said quietly, his voice almost a soundless whisper.

"About?" she asked, answering in the same low voice.

"My daughter. Is she bothering you?"

"No, not at all."

"What were you talking about?"

"Fathers. Why?"

Nigel sat back in his chair and saying nothing more, Justine started to move past him. "I do the best I can."

His softly muttered words made her realize that he had a few doubts about himself. That vulnerability—admitting that he had it—struck her. She put both hands on his desk and leaned forward, coming closer to him than she knew he expected. His eyes widened.

"You do better than most men," Justine said. "She's a good kid and very . . ."

Justine wasn't a woman with a big vocabulary, and somehow calling Piper wise for her age didn't strike her as the right thing to say. "You are doing a good job with her. She's safe, and that's all that really matters."

Nigel laughed a bit at that. "Safety is important. That's why I hired you."

"I'm good at my job."

"That's obvious."

Justine straightened to walk away, but he stopped her again, putting his hand on her arm this time, not grabbing her. His fingers feathered over the exposed skin of her wrist, and she felt a tiny shiver slide up her arm. She glanced back down at him. His eyes were narrowed as he looked at his big hand on her arm.

"Thank you for being so good at your job."

It was the one thing she'd always had, and she realized that while the restlessness inside of her wanted something else, this was really all she could ever be. This job, this thing she'd become to survive. And for the first time since she'd learned that Baron Industries was their client, she was glad of it.

The rest of the flight was smooth, but Nigel was distracted and restless. Ha! He was horny and he couldn't concentrate on anything except the way Justine had felt in his arms. He wanted her back there again.

But not now. He had a factory to open, and another matter to take care of deep in the jungle, that no one, save Jenkins, knew about. Usually the excitement of doing the odd jobs he did for the government kept him on his toes. But this one had gotten out of hand and the office he worked for had suggested he hire Liberty Investigations. He had the odd feeling that his identity had been compromised.

He'd almost left Piper at home. For the first time since her mother's death, he'd thought about separating the two of them. But in the end, he still felt that his daughter would be safer with him in the Amazon Basin than tucked away in their home in the States.

Jenkins's injury had shaken him. He liked the work he did for the government because it was usually pretty straightforward, and it gave him a thrill to be doing something with a hint of danger involved.

But the price of that thrill was more than he realized when he'd visited Jenkins in the hospital, and found the man barely conscious.

His mobile phone rang and he glanced at the caller ID before answering it. It was Derrick Baron. Nigel was half tempted to let it go to voicemail, but he didn't.

"This is Nigel."

"It's Derrick. We have a situation in the office."

"I have confidence you can handle it."

Derrick cleared his throat and Nigel waited to see what the other man was going to say.

"I . . . um . . . I already did handle it."

"Good. Are there any problems that need my attention?"

"No. Not yet. But I wanted to make you aware—

"Derrick."

"Yes?"

"I trust you. You are the one I put in charge. Whatever decisions you make, I know you have the best interests of Baron in mind."

Nigel heard Derrick exhale. "I do. Thanks, Nigel."

"No problem."

Nigel hung up the phone and focused on work. Justine moved about the cabin in that vigilant way of hers. She stopped once in a while to talk to Constance or Piper, but for the most part, she remained focused on her job. Considering that was what he was paying her for, he knew he had no reason to be annoyed.

But he was.

He knew that the annoyance was basic, a simple masculine instinct that made him want to demand her attention. To have her fixated on him the way he was on her. Even though he was pretending not to be.

He actually felt the layers of civilization peeling away each time he watched her pace past his desk. With each trip she made up and down the aisle, he felt his skin tighten until he had balled his hands into fists to keep from reaching for her again.

Justine stopped in front of him, and for just a moment, he thought about picking her up and carrying her to the bedroom at the back of the plane.

"Can we speak privately?"

"Yes," he said.

Piper and Constance were seated in the front of the plane, and he gestured to the captain's chair next to his desk.

"I mean in the bedroom."

He arched one eyebrow at her. "Sure."

Nigel followed Justine as she walked down the aisle and into the plush room. Piper's favorite stuffed bunny was sitting on the pillow.

"I'd like to go over a few things before we land."

"Yes?"

"I've just learned that the manifest of passengers has been sent ahead of us with our flight plan."

"Is that a problem?" Nigel asked, knowing that with the heightened security measures that had been enacted since September 11, it was impossible to fly into any foreign country anonymously.

"It is if your enemies have any access to the immigration office."

"What do you recommend?"

"I have a Kevlar vest for you and Constance to wear. I didn't think to bring one small enough for Piper. But I called my partners and they will have one for her when we land in Lima."

"Flying into Lima isn't the most direct route," Nigel said. With his private plane, he was used to flying to the exact location where he needed to be. Lima was a good day's ride from Cusco. And from Cusco, it was half day's drive in a Humvee to get to the factory.

"Safety is my concern, Nigel. Not directness. We'll get you there in one piece."

"I wasn't complaining."

"I know. I just . . ."

"What?"

"Nothing."

But Nigel sensed it wasn't nothing. He and Justine had crossed a line earlier. One that client and bodyguard should never cross. It didn't matter that he was thinking about crossing it again. Right now, all that mattered was that Justine was shaken because of it.

And now he knew that he needed to pull back. His being distracted wasn't a problem, because if he missed a detail at work no one would die. If Justine was distracted, there was a very good chance that she'd lose that vigilance she had—and that could mean Piper's life.

"Is that all?"

She glanced at him with that tough-as-nails gaze of hers, shaking her head. "Put on the vest and make sure Constance does as well."

He nodded and watched her leave the room.

Justine's BlackBerry twittered as soon as she stepped out of the bedroom. She glanced at the caller ID screen before answering. The job, she thought, knowing that was what she needed to be concentrating on, instead of thinking about Nigel and that huge bed in the back room.

"What's up, Anna?"

"Hello, Justine. I've been trying to find out more about the group of mercenaries who we believe are responsible for the attack on Jenkins, but so far I've gotten nowhere." Anna said.

"What about Sam and his contacts?" Justine asked. Mercenaries weren't the team's favorite people to go up against. It was easier to deal with adversaries who were fighting for a cause or their beliefs, instead of someone who killed simply for money. Justine had no problem with killing to protect someone for a cause, but for money . . . that had always pissed her off.

Like you had no allegiance. She shook her head to clear it, as she realized Anna was saying something.

"Sam's contacts are being quiet about this one. Other than saying they believe it was a group of mercenaries who attacked Jenkins, they've said little else," Anna said.

"If Sam can't get any info, that must mean there's more to this than the environmental concerns of some local villagers," Justine said.

"That's my thought as well. I don't like the variables we are dealing with. Bringing a kid into this situation is irresponsible. Is there any way you can talk him into sending the girl back to the States?"

"I doubt it." Nigel had been adamant about keeping Piper with him. And she admired him for that, but like Anna, she knew that with the variables they would encounter on this mission, having a kid along was a complication they just didn't need. Piper could tip the scales in the mercenaries' favor so easily.

"Doesn't he care about his daughter at all?" Anna asked.

Justine knew that Nigel did care very much for Piper. But she didn't want to explain all that to Anna. "He cares a lot for her."

"Well, then play on that," Anna said.

"Do you know something you aren't telling me?" Justine asked as she realized there was a real determination behind Anna's desire to keep Piper from entering Peru.

"Nothing concrete, just some rumblings from my contacts, and . . ."

"What?"

"A feeling in my gut that the kid is a vulnerability."

"A child's entire existence is fragile," Justine said, her mind drifting back to her own childhood for a second. She was caught between this conversation with Anna and her own past.

"True enough, but we aren't usually responsible for a child. I don't like it." There was vehemence in Anna's voice, and Justine remembered that her friend had been kidnapped when she was a young teenager.

"Is it bringing back memories of your kidnapping?"

"No," Anna said. But there was a note in her voice that said otherwise. Justine wanted to find out more about the past that Anna rarely mentioned, but she didn't like to talk about her own childhood, so she kept quiet.

"Can you get a Kevlar vest for the kid?" Justine asked.

"Charity is working on it. We're going to try to get the head of immigration to process Nigel and his daughter into the country so that we can stay with them the entire time."

"Good. I'll contact you before we land so that I know where to direct them. Don't forget to include the nanny—Constance Wareham."

"I have her on the list. If there're any flags for immigration, I'll let you know."

Justine heard the sound of Anna's fingers moving over the keyboard as they spoke, and she knew that their other agent was checking on things at the same time. Talking to Anna was returning her sense of normalcy. Making her focus on the job again, and stop thinking about Nigel and how he'd felt when she'd landed on top of him. How he'd felt when she'd kissed him.

"Good. So that's all for now?" Justine said, instead of just hanging up like she usually would have. A part of her was reluctant to let Anna go. Because once again, she'd be back to dealing with Nigel, and the attraction between them that she had no clue how to handle.

"Yes. You okay?"

"Why wouldn't I be?"

"You don't sound like yourself."

"Neither do you," Justine said. She should have hung up. She'd been ignoring Nigel very nicely, but Anna was a different case. Turning the conversation back on her helped a bit. Justine closed her eyes and shut out the man who was disturbing her. Made him nothing more than a cardboard cutout. The client, nothing more. Who cared that he was a good father and he did things for Piper that her own dad had never done for her?

"I'm just ticked because I can't find the answers I've been looking for."

"Yeah, me too."

"Answers to what?"

"Nothing. I just meant my thing isn't any big deal," Justine said.

"Do you want to talk?"

"Hell, no. I'm not a talker."

Anna laughed. "No, you aren't. Charity is, though, and she's had a lot to say about Daniel."

Justine smiled. "Lucky you."

"I wouldn't go straight to lucky. If she mentions him one

more time, I'm going to scream. I mean literally, there's not a single subject I bring up that she doesn't turn back to him."

"I'm glad it's you and not me."

"Me, too. Otherwise, you two would probably be sparring."

Sparring sounded good to Justine right now. She needed the freedom that came from fighting. Talking, sitting, thinking about Nigel—those things were making her edgy. A good solid fight would loosen her up. Too bad there wasn't a dojo on the plane.

"True. See you on the ground," Justine said.

"Yes. I'll email or text the information from immigration once I receive it."

"Good. Bye."

"Justine?"

"Hmm?"

"Whatever's going on in your head . . . you need to get over. No matter what Sam thought at the beginning, this isn't going to be a cakewalk."

Justine hung up without replying. She knew that better than anyone. Pocketing her BlackBerry, she looked down the aisle of the plane and saw Piper and Constance sitting quietly, and realized then that she wasn't going to let anything hurt Piper or Nigel, or even Constance, for that matter.

For once, it wasn't just because she was being paid to do a job. A part of it was because of Piper, and helping kids who were in mortal danger had always been important to her. Another bigger part had to do with Nigel.

Not because Nigel was one hell of a kisser or because Piper reminded her of the girl she'd once been. She was going to ensure their safety because it was her job, and without that, she had no idea who she was.

Chapter Five

Piper was distracted and cranky after almost eleven hours on the plane. Constance was keeping her close, and Nigel was a bit on edge since Anna and Charity had entered the plane on the ground in Lima. He'd seen the censure in the eyes of Justine's team. Fuck them. He knew how to take care of Piper. And no one could protect her like he could.

The team tested their earpiece mikes, then took up positions in the plane. They'd all donned the Kevlar vests under their clothing. Right now they were waiting for the Immigration representative to arrive and clear them into the country.

"Pedro Maldano will be here in a few minutes. He will serve as an escort for our party to Immigration. Entering Peru isn't a big deal for any of us since our countries are on good terms with the current government," Charity said.

The tall blond woman was stunningly beautiful, but Nigel realized he noticed her looks only as a matter of fact. He wasn't attracted to the buxom blonde at all. He had never really gone for obvious beauty.

Anna was seated next to Piper, Charity stood in front of the door, and Justine was positioned to his left. "How much longer do you think this will take?"

Justine glanced over at him. "I have no idea. Do you have somewhere you need to be?"

"No. I think Piper's going to have a meltdown in a few minutes, though," he said, glancing at his daughter, who was swinging her bunny rabbit around by its ears and staring at Constance with a belligerent look on her face.

"I . . . don't know what we can do. It will be worse for her in the long line at customs rather than waiting for the officials to come to us."

"I know," he said, rubbing his hand against the back of his neck. He felt itchy and restless. He needed to get off this plane and away from Justine. He wanted Piper safe in the secure housing on the Baron Industries compound.

Justine didn't say anything to him. He'd noticed that she'd shut down personally toward him and that was fine. He'd been treating her the same way, but now, seeing her with the other women, he realized how much he missed the feisty comments she'd made at first. Now she was nothing but an automaton doing her job, with all the emotion of the Terminator.

The pilot stepped out of the cockpit. "There is a black Mercedes parking next to the plane."

"Thanks, Mark," Charity said. "I'll go greet Pedro. Everyone stay back from the door."

Justine moved in front of him and Anna positioned herself in front of Piper.

"Why can't we leave, Daddy?"

"We have to wait until they are ready for us, Pip."

"How much longer?"

"Not too much," Nigel said.

"I want to get off the plane."

"Me, too," Justine said. "But we need to follow the rules of entry for this country."

Piper wasn't buying it, though, and Nigel saw the bratty look on his eight-year-old's face a second before she opened her mouth. "My daddy is a very important man. We shouldn't have to wait."

"Piper," Nigel said in a firm tone.

"It's true, Daddy," she said.

"If there were any way to get us off this plane more quickly, don't you think I'd do it?"

She nodded.

"Sit down next to Constance and be quiet."

"I don't—

"Piper?" Justine interrupted.

"Yes?"

"Remember how we talked about fathers earlier?"

Piper nodded.

"This is one of those times when, if we want to keep your father safe, we are just going to have to wait."

She bit her lower lip and hugged her stuffed bunny closer to her chest before sitting down next to Constance.

Nigel wasn't too sure he liked the way Justine had handled the situation, but Piper was sitting quietly now.

Nigel took Justine's arm to draw her back, but she evaded his grip. "I'd like a word with you."

"Not now."

"Yes, now."

"Nigel, Charity is almost done with Maldano, and he is coming onboard in a minute. We can talk later."

He felt like he imagined what his daughter had felt when Justine had silenced her. "Yes, we will."

Anna and Justine both palmed their weapons and moved to stand on either side of the cabin door.

Charity reentered the plane first, followed by a tall dark-skinned man. "Welcome to Peru, Mr. Carter. I'm Pedro Maldano."

Nigel stepped forward and offered the man his hand. The handshake was strictly three pumps up and down, and Pedro had a very firm handshake. Usually that meant the man Nigel was dealing with had a lot of integrity.

"Thank you. It's my pleasure to be here."

"And ours to have you," Pedro said. "We'll have you through customs in a short time, and then you are to be the guests of the minister of finance tonight. He has a guest home in Lima that he has prepared for you."

Alejandro Perez, the minister of finance, had bent over backward to be helpful since Jenkins was attacked. Nigel knew it was because the Peruvian government didn't want Baron Industries to pull out of building their factory.

"That's very kind of him," Nigel said.

He wasn't sure staying in the minister of finance's guest home was a smart idea, but for right now, he wanted to get through customs and get Piper safely in a car of their own. "This is my daughter, Piper, and her nanny, Constance Wareham."

"Welcome, ladies."

"Hola, Señor," Piper said, using the Spanish that Constance had taught her for the trip.

"Hola, Señorita Carter."

Nigel listened to his daughter exchange pleasantries in Spanish and looked over at Constance. She smiled at him. They were both so proud of Piper. Constance was skilled, and had functioned as so much more than a nanny in the years that she'd been with Nigel and Piper. She had become a part of their family.

"Let's go," Pedro said, and they all filed slowly off the plane. Pedro led the way, with Charity and Constance behind him, and Anna and Piper following. Nigel had just set his foot on the top step when a loud explosion rocked the ground.

Justine tackled Nigel and got him flat on the ground. The asphalt was hard and bit into her hands as she pushed herself up for leverage. Nigel was cursing softly under his breath next to her. Piper was crying, but not too loudly, and Charity reported that Constance had passed out.

Justine scanned the area around the plane to see where the threat was coming from. Maldano's car was in flames, burning at the end of the tarmac.

"Get the Carters to the car we secured," Charity said. "I'll stay here with Maldano until the officials arrive."

Justine tugged Nigel to his feet. He immediately turned to Piper, and Justine knew she'd have a struggle keeping him from his daughter, so she let him go, but covered him with her gun drawn. Anna was doing the same from the other side.

"What about Constance?" Nigel asked.

"Let's get you two to safety, and then we will worry about her. Charity won't let any harm come to her."

"Good. Where are we heading?" Nigel asked.

"That black sedan. Stay low and move fast. Anna has Piper, so don't hesitate. Keep moving."

"I can't do that. I need to make sure Piper is okay."

"Anna, take the lead. I've got your back." Justine pushed Nigel back down. "Stay low."

All the talking and waiting was making her nervous. They needed to get out of the open and away from the airport. "Go, Anna."

"I'm moving."

Anna had one hand on Piper's upper arm. The little girl had tear tracks drifting down her face, and clung to her stuffed rabbit with her other arm. Justine knew that Nigel was struggling to follow her orders. She felt him lurch toward his daughter, and understood his need to comfort her.

Anna moved swiftly but kept a pace that Piper could easily maintain. They were less than one hundred feet from the car when Justine heard a spray of gunfire from a semiautomatic weapon. Anna hit the deck once again, covering Piper's body with her own. Nigel was up and running toward his daughter before Justine could stop him.

She returned fire, though she struggled to see her target. She pulled her night-vision glasses from her side pocket and donned them, hitting a button on the side, enabling the thermal imaging.

"Anna?"

"I've got Piper and Nigel. We're moving toward the sedan again."

"I've got you covered. Haven't sighted the assailant yet."

"I . . ."

"Stay with Nigel," Charity said. "Maldano is hit and Constance is conscious. I'm going to leave the two of them here, and I'll hunt the assailant."

"Affirmative," Justine said.

"Anna, get to the car and pick up Constance and Maldano," Justine said. "I'll cover you."

"Affirmative."

Justine kept her attention focused and laid a burst of ground fire to cover Anna and the Carters as they ran for the sedan.

"We're in. The driver has been shot."

"Fuck. Get out of the car. It may have been tampered with."

Anna was cursing simultaneously. Justine saw the car door open out of her peripheral vision, but kept her own gaze sharp. Anna and the Carters were back out of the car in seconds and moving toward her. Justine wished she had her damn assault rifle instead of the Beretta, but they hadn't anticipated this kind of trouble at the airport.

"I'm going silent," Charity said.

"Affirmative," Justine said. "We're getting back on the plane. We'll get airborne and decide what to do next."

Running away didn't sit right with her, but Justine and the

team's first priority was to keep Nigel Carter and his daughter alive.

Constance ran over to Piper and wrapped the little girl in her arms. Nigel put his arm around both of them. Justine saw the anger and fear on his face. Dammit, this was a mess. They needed to take control of the situation. "Do you have an alternate route out, Anna?"

"Yes. In the hangar. We'll have to go together. I don't like leaving anyone out here."

"Then let's go. I'll cover these three. Do you want to get Maldano?"

"I can get myself," Maldano said. "My men should be here in a moment."

"Someone blew up your car . . . I'm not sure you should trust your men."

"I trust them, Ms. O'Neill, the way you trust your partners."

"Well, until they arrive, we're going to the hangar. We can defend our position better from there," Justine said.

There was no more fire from the assailant and nothing from Charity. Justine was edgy; she was better at going after a target in the dark than Charity. That wasn't to say Charity wasn't very good at the task. Only that Justine preferred action to guarding.

"We're heading toward the hangar. Stay low and keep moving. Constance, put Piper down and let her walk."

"I won't. My baby is tired and scared. I can run with her like this."

Justine didn't have time to argue with the other woman. "Nigel?"

"Let her carry Piper."

"Let's go then. Follow Anna."

Anna moved quickly over the tarmac, followed by Constance, then Maldano. Nigel moved swiftly, and kept his eyes on his daughter and her nanny.

Justine swept her gun from left to right, moving quickly through the darkness. In the distance, she saw lights approaching. Maybe Maldano's men. She wasn't waiting on them for the rescue. Justine knew Anna wasn't, either.

They needed to get the Carters and the nanny to safety. Justine entered the hangar just as Constance and Piper got in a second car. A burst of gunfire from behind her caused Justine to turn. She returned fire this time, able to see her target.

Nigel was sick of getting shot at and watching his daughter cringe. As soon as Piper and Constance were in the car, he signaled the driver to leave. He wanted his daughter out of harm's way—NOW.

"Where do you need another weapon?" he asked, taking the Kimber .45 he had in a holster at the small of his back.

"Nowhere. Get your head down and stay put," Justine said.

She continued returning fire at the assailant, barely acknowledging his comments. He took a moment to survey the situation and then took a position between the two women. Maldano was on the other side of Anna.

The car seemed to have made a clean getaway, and knowing his daughter was safe, Nigel let go of the anger he'd been keeping bottled inside. He wanted these bastards dead.

He added his firepower to the mix, and heard Justine curse next to him. He saw a glimpse of a shadow to the right of the hangar entrance, and concentrated his shots there, hitting his target and watching the body drop to the floor.

He fired two more times before he spent his clip. "I'm out of ammo."

"What are you using?" Anna asked, her clipped British accent even more pronounced while they were under fire.

"Kimber Ultra Covert."

".45 caliber?" Justine asked.

"Yes."

She reached under her coat and tossed him a clip for the weapon. He popped it into his gun and continued defending their position. "You're only good for another thirteen rounds. Make them count."

"I will," he said.

They didn't have the firepower to hold the garage area for long, and he had the feeling the women knew it, too. "Nigel, stay here and continue shooting. I'm going around behind them."

Nigel nodded. Justine handed him a second gun. A Glock .9 mm and an extra ammo clip. "When you run out . . ."

"You had better be in position by then," he said.

"I will be."

Justine disappeared, and Anna started firing a second gun so that the assailants didn't realize their numbers had changed. The firefight was less intense, as if the other side were being judicious with their firepower as well.

How long could this last, he wondered. He'd only been in one other exchange like this. He was an executive, for the love of God. And not at all used to dealing with this type of situation.

But he'd grown up in Essex—a rough neighborhood in London—and had learned early on how to survive. Getting in touch with that lad wasn't all that hard. The years of civilization were stripped away. The anger he felt at Piper being threatened turned to determination as he honed it into the concentration he needed to ensure that he survived. That Justine survived. Having got his daughter to safety, it was now imperative that he keep Justine safe, as well.

It didn't matter that she was a trained professional, and that he'd hired her to keep his daughter safe. He knew now that ignoring her on the plane had been a mistake. He wanted her.

It sucked that the realization became clear to him as he was waiting for her to reappear, not sure if either of them was going to live to see morning. That wasn't true. He was Nigel Carter, a rough and tough street kid who'd made more of his life than anyone thought he had the right to. He certainly wasn't going to die in a hangar in Lima, Peru.

"Can you fire and move?" Anna asked.

"I can," Nigel replied.

"I, as well," Pedro said.

"We'll move forward on the count of three. Justine and Charity are in position, so all we have to do is close the net. Draw them in. Ready?"

"Yes," he said.

"Sí."

"We move on three." Anna counted down and they all moved, fanning forward while maintaining their cover. It was difficult, but the instinct to survive and win was one that Nigel was used to. And it was very strong at this moment.

A bullet whizzed past him from the left, almost hitting him in the shoulder. He ducked, but a second bullet tore through his upper arm, the pain a deep burning. He dropped his weapon and picked it up with his other hand. He wasn't as accurate with his left hand, but he could still fire with it.

He turned to the left and waited a moment, forcing away the pain in his arm. He held his breath and saw movement in the corner. Positive he had the position of the man who'd just shot him, he returned fire and was satisfied when he heard the sound of a weapon hitting the ground.

Nigel ran forward, hitting the man in the gut and knocking the breath from him. He brought his hand down on the side of the man's neck, aiming for his carotid artery and finding it. The man collapsed at his feet, and Nigel glanced to his right to see that Anna had subdued two other men.

"Do you have anything to bind his hands?"

She tossed him a pair of flex cuffs. He bound the unconscious man's hands.

"Nice job," Anna said.

"Thanks. How'd Pedro do?"

"Just as well as you," Anna said.

They searched the rest of the garage area and found two dead bodies, one of which Nigel was certain was the man he'd hit when he'd first pulled his Kimber. He looked down into the man's eyes because taking a life wasn't something that should ever be done lightly.

Nigel reached down and closed the man's eyes, then got to his feet.

They stepped outside the building, guns drawn, and found Justine and Charity with four men bound between them. "This area is secure."

"The building is, too," Nigel said.

Justine walked over to him, looking from the weapon held loosely in his hand back to his eyes.

"Good job, Nigel."

He nodded to acknowledge her thanks. But inside, he realized that this was her world. She was at home here and totally comfortable with the violence and blood. At one point in his life, he had been, too, but he no longer was. He wondered if he ever would be again.

Chapter Six

Maldano's men arrived with local law enforcement to take the assailants into custody. They were known terrorists in the area, and after questioning them, Charity found out they weren't targeting Nigel. They had been following Maldano, looking for a high-profile person to kidnap and further their cause.

"Have you talked to Constance?" Nigel asked, coming up behind her. His accent was crisp. He looked tired and didn't really seem like an executive at this moment. It was as if the firefight had striped away the layers of posh sophistication that he'd had before. Now she saw there was more to him, and that intrigued her.

"No. Our driver should have checked in, though. Let me see if Anna has."

Nigel followed her across the room. It was the kind of place that didn't have any real décor to mention, unless one considered late '60s metal desks and cracked framed prints décor.

"Have you heard from Jesse?" Justine asked Anna. She wanted Nigel away from her. She was ultra-aware of him walking behind her. She had wanted to reach for him after the shooting was over. Whatever attraction had sparked between them on the plane had grown while she'd been defending them. While she'd watched him show his measure of the man he was.

He wasn't a useless executive, which she'd already begun to suspect. And she wanted more from him. She was wondering if that kiss on the airplane had been a fluke. Had he really felt right in her arms? Was she completely losing it?

The heat in Lima must be making her crazy, she thought.

"No," Anna said, her accent just as crisp as Nigel's. "As I just told you ten minutes ago."

"You haven't followed up?" Justine asked, her own tone sharp. She didn't like being taken to task by anyone, especially her partners. Her own temper was short as she tried to figure out what was going on with her emotions about Nigel. She didn't do this. She wasn't the type of woman who got her panties in a twist over a *man*.

"No, I haven't. I have been dealing with the local authorities and explaining our body count. Would you rather have done that for me?"

She shook her head, running her hand through her short mane. "Sorry. Will you check on his GPS? He's not answering his cell."

"No problem," Anna said, pulling out her small minicomputer. "Give me a second."

"What does it mean that you can't get in touch with the driver?" Nigel asked.

His shirt was torn and he had the gun tucked into his waistband. He was so different from the man she'd first seen earlier.

"It could mean nothing. Just bad satellite reception."

"But you don't think so?" he asked.

"I have no idea. I just want to make sure we cover all our bases. Someone threatened you. Your daughter should be safe, but I won't be happy until we know where she is."

"She's with Constance. That should be enough of a reassurance."

"You can't get in touch with her," Justine said. "How reassured are you?"

He scowled at her.

"Listen, I'm not trying to wind you up. We just need to cover all the bases. That's why you hired us."

"You're right. I know that, but I just want to know that Piper is safe so I can relax."

"I doubt that will be enough for you to relax. Was this your first firefight?"

Nigel looked away from her and she realized he was about to tell her a lie. That newly awakened part of her felt a twinge of disappointment. She'd almost started to believe that Nigel was different than other men.

"Don't bother answering," she said, talking over whatever he'd been about to say.

"Why not?"

"I'm not interested in being lied to."

She saw the surprise on his face. "Not many people would call me a liar to my face."

"Maybe they have a higher tolerance for falsehoods than I do."

"Or maybe they just don't consider evasion lying."

"Then you must be surrounded by idiots," Justine said. She was on edge. She should get away from their client and just take a breather. But Charity was still talking to the authorities, and Anna was still doing a computer track of Jesse's whereabouts.

So no one else was available to take care of Nigel, and leaving him alone wasn't an option. No matter that these assassins weren't after Nigel—there was an enemy out there gunning for him. And no matter how angry he made her right now, he was her responsibility.

"Justine?"

"Yes?"

"I think you need to relax."

"That's not going to happen," she said. "I'm not really one of those people who's all smiley faces."

He barked out a laugh, and she felt a little bit of the tension that had been riding her slide away.

"No kidding."

"Listen, Anna will get back to us when she finds something, but I need to get out of this room. You'll be safe if you stay here. Okay?"

"Where are you going?"

"Just outside. I need to breathe."

She walked away before he could say anything. Before the spark of attraction that had once again flared to life had a chance to burn any brighter. Because Nigel Carter was so different than any other man she'd met, he was making her realize there was an entire part of herself as a woman she didn't know.

The night air was heavy and warm as he stepped outside the Quonset hut. He needed a stiff drink or a fight, he thought. Justine had almost given him the fight, but at the last minute she'd dropped back and retreated. He was edgy and restless. No doubt from having killed.

He'd forgotten his gang days. Forgotten the emotions that went with violence. And they weren't always the ones he expected. There had been the thrill, and the excitement and adrenaline rush during the actual fight, but now he had the excess still running through him.

His daughter was out of radio contact, but safe. Constance would protect Piper with her life, and the staff at Liberty Investigations had proven they hired only the most skilled.

He didn't question why he wasn't able to relax . . . he

scanned the area outside the hut and found the reason. Pacing angrily back and forth. Hands held loosely at her sides. Those combat boots of hers making a solid sound with each step she took. She had on a shoulder holster and two guns strapped to her back. There was a knife sheath at her waist and as she turned to face him, Nigel realized he'd never wanted a woman more.

"Has Anna heard anything?" Justine asked.

"Not yet," he said.

He closed the gap between them. The lights outside the hut were the kind that didn't cast a shadow, so they were both utterly exposed. He didn't mind. Not really. Physically, he wasn't hiding anything from her. And he knew instinctively that Justine wasn't, either. She wasn't the kind of woman to use subterfuge.

"Then what are you doing out here?"

"Following you."

"That's dangerous."

"I think you can keep me safe from my enemies . . . besides, we're at the security compound."

"I wasn't referring to your enemies."

He arched one eyebrow at her. Maybe he wasn't the only one spoiling for a fight. "Are you threatening me?"

"Of course not . . . I'm just saying there are dangers everywhere."

"I know that," he said, thinking of his own life. As a kid he'd thought having money would ensure that he'd be safe. But then Piper had come along, and he'd realized that he'd always be vulnerable.

God, he missed that little girl. He absolutely needed for her to be safe. And waiting here . . . was killing him.

"Sure you do," Justine said.

"Wait until you have a kid, and then talk to me. You have no idea how vulnerable that makes a man."

Justine froze. "I had a kid sister . . . I do understand what you mean."

"What happened?"

"She . . . she and I lost touch."

There was more to this story than she was saying. He could see that and he wanted to keep pushing, but his gut said that now wasn't the time.

"Recently?"

"No . . . a long time ago. Let's go back inside and see if Anna has found anything."

"I thought you needed to breathe."

"I can't do that while you're out here."

He touched the side of her face; she tipped her head to the side for a second, leaning into him, and then seemed to realize what she'd done and stood up straighter.

"Nigel, you make me crazy."

"Good," he said, leaning down and claiming the kiss he needed. It was the only thing that felt right at this instant. She didn't melt against him, but then Justine wasn't really the melting type of woman. Instead, she caged his head in her hands, holding on to him as she tried to take control of the kiss.

He let her. At six-four he was a big man, and most women just naturally let him take the lead, but that wasn't in Justine's makeup. And as she angled her head and thrust her tongue deep into his mouth with blatant sexuality, it was all he could do not to grab her waist and draw her to him, lift her off her feet and wrap those slender legs around his hips so he could go where his cock demanded. He needed to have her wrapped around him.

Completely at his mercy.

He took control of the kiss, thrusting his tongue back into her mouth and sweeping his hands down her back. He cupped her butt and lifted her off her feet. She gasped. He felt it, and for a second he thought she was going to knee him, but then she wrapped one thigh around his hips and let him take her weight.

He held her to him and plumbed her mouth, sucking at her lips and tasting her. Tasting her courage and her femininity and craving more. He couldn't get enough of this one woman, and that never happened to him.

Was it simply the danger? The fact that they'd faced death together that made him want her like he'd wanted no other? Or was it something more?

Hell, why was he trying to think when his dick was influencing him? Maybe this was nothing more than a raging case of lust. She was different; she was hot and she was a challenge.

He tried to find her skin underneath her T-shirt, but it was tucked in and there was an arsenal strapped to her body. He groaned.

She pulled his shirt from his waistband and he felt the touch of her small hands against his chest. He looked around for privacy. He carried her to the side of the Quonset hut, turning so that her back was against the side wall and they were out of view of anyone who came to the door.

He let her legs drop and put his arms on either side of her head as he leaned into her. Letting his body come to rest on hers. He reached for her breasts, but she exploded into action, her knee coming up between his legs and her hand hitting him in the throat.

He doubled over in pain and stepped back. "What the hell?"

Justine didn't have time to explain. She was wrapped in a cloud of the past. As soon as Nigel had placed her body between his and the wall, the present had fallen away. She remembered . . . Franklin Baron, and the way he'd cornered her in that long hallway on the third floor.

She had reacted with instinct and now . . . she backed away from Nigel and tried to get a grip on where she was. Dammit, she needed to get away. She moved farther from him, but he started toward her.

"Justine?"

She heard Anna calling as if from a distance. She couldn't take her eyes off Nigel. She didn't want to turn her back on him, but the reality of what she'd done filtered through her fear-and-panic-dazed mind. She stepped around Nigel and put the wall of the hut at her back.

"Give us a minute," Nigel said.

"What's up?"

"Nothing. We need a minute."

Justine knew she should step in and speak up, do something to alleviate the worry she saw on Anna's face, but all she could do was stare at both of them. Keep her back to the wall and let the flashback of her past play through her mind. She knew it wouldn't last forever. That it would end and she'd be okay, but right now, keeping her screams deep inside was really all she could do.

"Justine?" Anna asked.

"Go."

Anna disappeared back inside and she was left alone with Nigel. "You, too."

"I'm not going anywhere until I'm sure you're okay," he said.

He was still a bit pale, and she knew she owed him an explanation for kneeing him, but she had no idea where to start. This was precisely why she never got involved with men. She kept her sexual urges to herself because she really wasn't comfortable with them.

And now she knew that the legacy from Franklin Baron was pain. Not just for her, but for anyone who came in contact with her.

She started shaking and realized she was on the edge of completely losing it.

"What can I do, love?"

She just shook her head, but he took a step toward her and she realized he wasn't going to leave her alone. She moved around him and stepped to the left so that he was between the building and her. Maybe she could play off her reaction as some kind of claustrophobia.

But lying went against her grain and Nigel deserved better from her.

"Is it me?"

She shook her head "I can't talk about it. I need to put that," she said, gesturing to the wall area, "behind me for right now."

He nodded. "I'll keep my hands to myself."

She didn't want him to, but she knew now that she wasn't going to be able to experience the kind of relationship with Nigel that she'd been half-hoping to. She'd been hoping . . . Oh, my God. She really had been hoping she was normal. That with Nigel she could be a normal woman.

"I think that would be best," she said, even though inside she felt like crying. Which was silly and ridiculous because she was too tough for tears. She always had been.

Why then would this man with the tough attitude make her feel like she was losing something? Losing a part of herself?

"We better go see what Anna found," she said. "I'll follow you."

She finally realized that she'd essentially forgotten she was the bodyguard—Nigel's bodyguard. She'd left him unprotected while she'd been kissing him, and then later as well.

"Let's get you back inside."

Nigel didn't say anything else, just walked in front of her into the hut. When they got inside, the lights seemed bright and there was a strangeness to the normalcy of the room. She walked over to her partners and tried to slip back into work mode, but something had changed inside her.

Goddamn Sam Liberty. She knew working with someone from Baron Industries was going to be a mistake. And now she had confirmation it was.

She was like a robot . . . no, an actress pretending she was still who she'd been, but that skin had been ripped away, and in its place was someone who didn't know who she was.

"Justine?"

"Yes."

"Did you hear what I said?" Anna asked, her accent clipped.

"Sorry, no. What?"

"I said we can't get anyone on the phones and the car has stopped moving. We need to get Nigel to the safe house while we go to the car."

"No," Nigel said. "I'm going after my daughter. If both Constance and your driver aren't answering their phones, something is wrong."

"Exactly," Anna said, giving her a strong look.

"Right. Nigel, we can't keep you safe in an area that may have turned hostile. Let Anna go after the car."

"I will not. And I'm tired of talking about it. Let's go before another minute passes. For all we know, Piper could be in peril."

"Fine, we'll all go, but you need to realize that if you won't listen to us, we can't keep you safe."

Nigel gave her a hard, cutting look and she knew that something had changed between them. Of course it had.

"You didn't keep my daughter safe," he said.

"You said the nanny would be protection enough," Justine said, before realized that she was deflecting. It wasn't his fault. They should never have allowed him to bring the girl. "Forget I said that. Arguing isn't going to do us any good."

Justine walked to the door and heard Nigel fall into step behind her. She pulled her gun and checked the clip before she opened it. No more rookie mistakes. She was going to be all about the job and forget about the woman Nigel had made her wish she could be.

"Wait."

She shook her head. "There is nothing more to discuss here. Your daughter's life is in danger and the clock is ticking. I think we both know—

He jerked her to a stop and she turned, ready to attack, stopping at the last moment as she realized her emotions were running high and she was spoiling for a fight.

For a fight, or something else physical. Oh, God, she wanted him. This was more than just curiosity about kissing a man. She had serious case of lust for Nigel Carter, and that was what was bothering her the most about Piper's disappearance.

She couldn't impress men the way other women could. Justine knew she had only her skills as a bodyguard to back her up, and she'd let him down.

She'd failed both Nigel and Piper, and as she pulled free of Nigel's grip and walked away, she realized she had failed herself.

Chapter Seven

Nigel was frustrated and worried about the women in his life—Piper, Constance, and Justine. Piper was such a big concern that he couldn't focus on his anger and worry. Instead, he focused on action. Going to Piper, getting her back by his side. Once he did, everything would be okay.

Constance was a concern only because he knew that she was with Piper and if she wasn't answering her phone . . . she would have to be dead. Constance always answered, even if she had a fever of 104 and was on her way to the emergency room.

Justine . . . she was the closest woman to him at the moment, and the one he focused on. He had no idea what had happened earlier, and as he sat behind her in the Hummer Utility Vehicle as they drove out of the city of Lima, he let himself dwell on thoughts of Justine. Because if he didn't, he was going to lose it.

Piper was way too young to be alone and scared, and every time he thought about his daughter, he started picturing horrible scenarios.

"Why are we leaving the city?" he asked as the lights of Lima faded in the distance.

"We are tracking the GPS signal in Jesse's phone," Justine said.

"The house we were to stay at—

"We know where it was. Something must have gone wrong," Anna said. She was sitting in the passenger seat and following the signal on her small computer. The women were ultra-efficient and seeing Justine like this underscored the fact that something had happened outside that was more than just the kiss.

He couldn't understand her reaction. The only explanation he could come up with was fear, but that emotion didn't fit with the woman driving with skill and confidence. In fact, the only explanation he could come up with made him feel ridiculous even thinking it.

She couldn't have been afraid of him or of any man. She had the skills to flatly take a man down. He was still a bit sore and tender between his legs. But that didn't stop him from wanting her.

It was more than just lust. Lust would have died when she'd reacted the way she had earlier. But instead, he now felt an insane desire to cuddle her. She was as prickly as a porcupine, and all he could think about was wrapping his arms around and holding her until she told him what had spooked her.

"Stop staring at me," Justine said.

"I'm watching the road," he said. It was dark outside and her features were illuminated by the dashboard, so delicate and feminine. Another dichotomy. The pixie features and petite body that housed a firecracker, kick-ass woman.

This was the worst possible time to be feeling anything like this, and yet he knew if he'd met Justine under normal circumstances, he would have brushed right by her and let his job consume him. But here in Peru, there was . . . only a situation he didn't want to lose himself in.

It was odd to think that his attraction to Justine might be the less dangerous of the two situations.

"Stop."

For a second, he thought she meant his thoughts, but he quickly realized there was a car on the side of the road. The same one that he had made sure Piper was safely ensconced in earlier this evening.

He had his door open and was out of the Hummer before it had completely stopped. "Nigel!"

He didn't heed Justine's call, though he knew she wanted him to stop. He was pulled toward the car, running flat out, and ripped open the back door to find the backseat empty.

"Bloody hell," he said. The coppery smell of blood registered, and he glanced to the front seat, where he saw Jesse slumped back in the seat. He had bled from two wounds, one in the chest and one in the neck.

There was no sign of blood in the backseat, and when Anna moved Jesse's body, he realized the women were just as shocked as he was by what had happened.

He paid little attention to the women and what they were doing, and climbed into the back of the car and searched for anything left behind. Piper's notebook was on the floor.

The little sketchbook that she'd drawn a picture of Justine in earlier. He flipped through the pages, searching for a note, or something from Piper. But she was nine and too young to think of that.

"This seems like it was an ambush," Justine said. "But I still don't like having you out here."

"Where should I go?" This entire situation was out of hand. Sam Liberty was going to know just how displeased he was with the service he was getting.

"Our vehicle. That way I can keep an eye on you and make sure that you are safe. What'd you find?"

"Piper's sketchbook."

"Try not to disturb anything. Anna is going to use our mobile crime scene processing kit to check for fingerprints and DNA."

"Sorry. I'm worried about my daughter. I'd think you guys would be, too."

"Of course we are. But we also need to know what happened here."

"What do you mean?"

"Well, we need to know why Jesse pulled off the road here."

"Are there other tracks?"

"I'm going to check on them once you are secure."

"I'll go with you."

"It's dark outside, Nigel, and I don't know that there isn't a sniper waiting out there for you."

"What do you know, Justine? Because so far, my daughter has been kidnapped, and that's not exactly what I hired you guys for."

"You said she'd be safe with Constance. She worked for you."

"Pointing the finger is the first sign that you know you aren't providing good service."

"Believe what you want, but Jesse was shot in the back of the head, and we think he may have pulled over because someone directed him to."

Justine was tired of things not going according to plan. Liberty Investigations was known for quality. But since they'd landed in Peru, nothing was working the way they liked for it to.

That mess with Maldano, and now Piper being missing, made her want to find the person who kidnapped the child and take justice into her own hands. Constance had been vetted twice—once when Nigel had hired her, and again when they'd taken on working with Nigel. If she had been working for someone else, they should have caught it.

If she wasn't working both sides, then there was a good chance the nanny was dead, which meant Piper was on her own. And how long she would survive was anyone's guess. Justine knew from personal experience how strong a nine-year-old girl could be.

"What are you implying?"

"Nothing but what we know. Jesse was shot in the back of the head . . . it could have been Constance. Either way, we know whoever has your daughter is more than likely the killer."

Nigel blanched, balled his hands into fists, and punched the back of the seat with enough force to rock the car. Justine took a step back. She'd give him a moment to process everything.

She took the Maglite and left Nigel alone. "I'm going to search for tire tracks."

"I've talked to Charity and she's on her way. Once she's here, we'll have you take Nigel to a safe house."

Justine didn't think he would go but kept that to herself. Instead, she went to search for tire tracks or boot tracks. They'd need to rule out the shoes they were all wearing. Standing on the asphalt, Justine skimmed the beam of light over the shoulder of the road, searching for anything out of the ordinary.

"Tell me how to help," Nigel said. His voice was low, almost hoarse. Her heart ached for him. She wanted to wrap her arms around him and offer comfort. To maybe make a few promises that she wasn't sure she could keep.

"Nigel—"

"Don't say anything. Just give me something to do so I don't have to think about Piper."

"Okay. We're searching for a track we can use. Trying to see if they were forced off the road by another car. Then we will try to identify the tire tracks and any prints left by the occupants."

"How will you know that they are the people who have Piper?"

"We won't. It's a process-of-elimination thing."

"That's it? That's the best you can do?"

"For right now. Do you have a GPS tracker in Constance's cell phone?"

"Yes. And one in Piper's stuffed bunny."

"Why didn't you mention that earlier?"

"I didn't think about it until this moment."

Justine knew it was a lie. She could hear it in his voice. Why would he hold on to that information?

"Sorry, it's my backup. No one knows about the bunny, not even Constance, and since she's a suspect . . ."

His voice cracked, and Justine couldn't keep silent a minute longer. "We'll find her."

"Don't make promises you can't keep."

"I'm not. One way or another we are going to find your daughter and the person who took her."

"And then what?"

"Then they'll wish they'd never taken her," Justine said.

"As soon as we are finished here, we need to get Anna the information on the GPS tracker you planted on Piper's stuffed bunny." Justine gave the ground one more look and saw a track she thought they might be able to get a good print from. And to be honest, she didn't want to wait to see if they could find Piper's GPS signal.

She bent down and marked the area before leading the way back to Anna.

"Did you find something?"

"I'm not sure. I marked a tire track, but before you check it out, Nigel just mentioned that Piper's stuffed animal has a GPS tracker in it."

"Nice. Let me get the computer, and let's see if we can find her."

"Was Jesse shot from the backseat?" Nigel asked.

"I can't tell yet. There is a lot of blood and I'm just starting to look at the splatter. I'll figure it out," Anna said.

Anna was good with crime scenes and could figure out whatever had happened. She'd let them know if Constance was who they should focus on. But right now, getting to Piper was the most important thing. They needed to move, if they could just find a signal to where she was.

Nigel gave Anna the information on how to log in to the GPS tracking system he had set up for Piper. And they all held their breath as she entered the information on her computer.

A map of the world came up, and they could see the maps processing as the satellite narrowed in on the GPS signal. They saw it start blinking and realized at once that it was moving.

"It's moving," Justine said, stating the obvious.

"Yes, heading toward . . . Cusco, I think. They just put in that new highway . . . let me see if we have a current map."

"Can we take your computer?"

"Of course, but you know this just means the stuffed animal is moving," Anna said.

"Piper wouldn't let that animal out of her hands," Nigel said.

Justine remembered how the little girl refused to be parted from either her nanny or her stuffed bunny. "Why not?"

"I told her that the bunny was . . . " he leaned in and spoke even softer. "I told her he was sent by an angel from her mother, and that the bunny would always watch over her."

Justine felt her throat tighten. Nigel was a good daddy. The kind of father that every child deserved, and as much as she regretted how deeply she was starting to care for him, she made a vow to ensure that they found Piper.

Nigel didn't feel embarrassed by what he'd admitted. Piper had needed something after her mother had died, and he'd done everything he could to make sure his daughter was taken care of. That she felt safe and loved and that he had every resource available to take care of her. Anna moved away to leave them alone.

"When her mom died, I had to do something."

"I understand. We have a choice, Nigel."

"We do?"

"Yes. We can stay here with Anna, process the scene, and then wait for Charity before tracking this signal, or we can go now. You should know there is a chance we could be following a dead trail."

"What's that mean?"

"That the GPS signal could be compromised and we'd be following the wrong trail."

"I'm the only one who knows about the bunny," he said.

"How confident are you of that?"

"99.9 percent sure. I ordered the GPS unit and put the tracking unit into the bunny myself. It's not stock-ordered."

"Then what do you want to do?"

"Go after Piper. I'm going to keep trying to reach Constance . . . can Anna find her signal from a cell phone number?"

"Depends on the wireless device. Anna?" Justine raised her voice. The other woman signaled to give her a moment.

"Before we leave . . ." he said.

"Yes?"

"We are going to be alone in the car for a long time . . . I want to know what happened back there at the airport. Why'd you knee me like that?"

Justine looked unsure for a moment. Then she turned away from him. She actually turned her back on him, and he knew she had to have forgotten that she was working, guarding him, because it was the first time she'd done it.

"You can trust me," he said, reaching for her. He caught her small shoulder under his hand and drew her back against him. She turned and it seemed almost nonchalant the way she stepped away from him.

"I don't really trust anyone," she said.

He didn't trust many people, but in business, he had to. He had to when he glanced at a signature on a contract, and knew that legally someone was bound to honor their own word.

"Not even your boss?" he asked, wording it carefully. "Or your teammates?"

"I trust Anna and Charity."

Interesting that it was the two women on her team that she mentioned first. He wasn't surprised because he was beginning to suspect that Justine had had a bad experience with men. He wondered if it was a broken heart.

"But not Sam?"

Justine glanced at him. "Why did you ask that?"

"Because of something he said when I talked to him."

"What did he say?"

"That you and Charity and Anna had the best instincts he had ever seen when it came to people, and if you three decided I wasn't telling the truth, he wouldn't take the job."

Nigel had been surprised—not many businessmen would turn down money. But Sam had been serious. And he had seen firsthand how competent the Liberty Investigations team was. Sam had assembled the best, and Nigel figured that was why he didn't have to worry too much about clientele.

"Sam knows we won't work for someone who lies to us. As far as that goes, I trust him not to send us a client we can't work for. But Sam keeps his own counsel on things, and occasionally he acts like he knows what's best for me."

That was interesting. "Like when?"

"Never mind. Trusting Sam isn't the same as trusting you."

"But you must know that I'm trustworthy."

"Belief and trust aren't the same things."

"I know that. But they usually go hand in hand," he said. He realized that he wanted more from her. He needed to know what had happened before because he was consumed with learning more about this woman. With knowing her for who she really was. And he was never going to be happy unless he had unraveled all of her secrets.

And somehow, talking to Justine eased the worry he felt for Piper.

"What do you want from me?" she asked.

"Right now, I just need to know why you kneed me. Because I still want you, and I don't want to take a chance on hurting or scaring you again."

She crossed her arms over her chest. "You didn't hurt me."

He noticed she didn't rule out being scared. With Justine, he was coming to realize he could learn more from what she didn't say sometimes.

"Was it something I did?"

"Yes."

"My hands on your body?"

"No."

"My tongue in your mouth?"

"For Pete's sake . . . no. I don't know why you are making such a big deal about this . . . I'm claustrophobic."

Yeah, right. He guessed there was probably an element of truth to what she said.

She walked away before he could ask her anything else, and that was fine with him. He watched her go, knowing that they'd be alone in the vehicle together and he'd get his answers then.

He was too tired emotionally to fight this attraction to Justine. He liked that the lust he felt for her distracted him from his worry about Piper. He knew he was using Justine, but he had the best of intentions where she was concerned.

And that would have to be good enough for now. Because

he knew he had no choice in the matter. He needed physical release, and Justine was the only woman he was interested in.

But lust had never controlled him, and he wasn't going to let it now. He could control his cock, and he wasn't going to let lust rule the day.

But as he watched her out of the corner of his eyes, he knew how hard that battle was going to be. Everything she did turned him on, and right now he needed the distraction of lust.

He turned away, disgusted with himself as he thought he might be using Justine to keep his mind off Piper. He wouldn't deny that he wanted Justine, and had since the moment she'd set foot in his office. But lusting after her and using her to distract him from the very real threat that he might not see his daughter again was something he wouldn't do.

"What is it?" she asked. Her voice was almost soft, and he knew she felt the same desperate need to get Piper back.

Nigel was very cognizant that his daughter had a way of winning over people who didn't expect to like kids. And he knew Justine was one of those people. As he watched her, he also knew that the attraction he had for her was so much more than a reaction to Piper being missing. It had to do with the woman she was, and how she called out to the man inside him.

Chapter Eight

The road between Lima and Cusco was a highway, and it was pretty easy to drive, which meant Justine really had nothing to distract her from the man sitting next to her in the passenger seat.

He was watching the flashing signal that was the only connection to his daughter. She saw his face get tight and she knew he was thinking about her, thinking about all the things that could happen to Piper.

"How'd you learn to shoot?" she asked abruptly.

When he glanced over at her, she wondered if he was going to lie to her this time the same way he had about killing a man.

"I learned from my mates."

"In the U.K.? They have some strict gun laws."

"Yeah, they do. These mates weren't exactly concerned about the law."

"You were some kind of street punk?" She couldn't really picture Nigel as anything other than what he was. She understood he was tough, and had the balls needed to kill someone in a life-threatening situation. But what she couldn't see was him as a person who didn't care about home and family. And usually the gangbangers she knew didn't care about anything but their gang.

"Not a punk . . . just a tough."

"A tough. How'd your folks feel about that?"

"My mother worked two jobs to support us. She wasn't really home that much. When I was fourteen, I started running with a gang, and I don't know that she ever noticed. She moved when I was sixteen, and I haven't seen her since."

Justine thought about her fractured family. How her mother had essentially left Justine behind after Justine had taken justice into her own hands. Socioeconomic scales didn't matter when it came to parents and kids. Was the picture she had in her head just some kind of fantasy? That image of a mom and a dad and kids that all loved each other—was that some kind of fairy tale?

Anna was close to her mother and brother, but Charity had a fractured family just like she did. And Justine realized Nigel did as well.

"Why are you staring at me like that?"

"Am I?" she asked, forcing her attention back to the road. "I should be watching where we are going."

He didn't say anything for a few minutes and then put his hand on her thigh. She jerked her foot off the gas before she could catch herself.

"Sorry," he said.

"It's fine."

"What were you thinking about?"

"Families."

"You said you had a sister."

"We didn't keep in touch."

"So, you're alone," he said.

She liked being alone, but realized a long time ago that people weren't comfortable with that idea. They thought she was strange or that she was a misanthrope. She liked people fine when they were doing their thing and not messing with her.

"I am."

"I was, too, until Piper. Have you ever thought about kids?"

Justine shuddered. She didn't mean to, but she couldn't stand the thought of bringing a child into the world who would be vulnerable. A child that might have to protect itself the way she had when her daddy died.

"I'm not very maternal."

"You don't have to be. I wasn't what anyone would have called father material before Piper was born."

"You weren't still in some street gang, were you?"

"No. But I was focused on work, on winning. You know, being the best and proving to the world, and I think my mother, that I didn't need them—or her."

Justine wondered if that was why she hadn't had kids. Was there a part of her that was afraid she'd end up being a crappy parent, like her mom?

"Did you prove it?" she asked. She really needed to stay focused on Nigel. It didn't matter what happened to her, she didn't want to talk to him or examine herself. Not now.

"I guess."

"You guess?"

"Yeah, I know it sounds lame, but one morning I realized I was trying to prove something to a woman who no longer existed."

"I don't understand."

"Well, I don't know the woman my mother is today, and in my mind, she always looks like she did when I was sixteen. I have changed a lot, and I have to imagine she did, too. So what was I trying to prove, you know?"

She nodded. She'd never thought of the past in those terms. Always when she thought of her mother and Franklin Baron, they were bigger than she was. They were young and uncaring. The kind of people who put their own selfish needs first. She had no idea if they would have changed . . .

Had she robbed the world of something by killing Franklin when she had? She always believed that he had molested others before her, and would do it again. That was simply the kind of man that Franklin Baron was.

She couldn't regret the fact he was no longer on earth. No longer breathing and ruining little girls' self-confidence

"You look very fierce sometimes."

"Do I? I can't help it."

"I didn't mean it was a bad thing. I think the person you are is interesting."

"I bet you don't know many women like me," she said. She wasn't the kind of woman who could have anything permanent with Nigel Carter. Despite his humble beginnings, he was a man who had changed to walk in a different world. He was an executive and a father and she was a murderer and a gun for hire. Those two things would never mesh.

Nigel didn't like talking about his past. It wasn't that he was ashamed of who he'd been, it was just that the past no longer defined him.

It was the man he was today that he was proud of. He hadn't always been respectable as a businessman, but since Piper's birth, he'd changed. He'd stopped thinking solely of himself and started focusing on the world around him.

Justine's cell phone rang.

"O'Neill."

"It's Sam. Are we on speaker? I need to talk to both of you."

"What's up, Sam?" Nigel asked.

"I'm working to get men in place with the mercenaries we think are working for the group that threatened you. Nigel, do you know of anyone else who might have a grudge against you?"

"Not really. I mean Derrick sometimes gets on my nerves, but I think he's okay with me. Why?"

"Because not one group I've had contact with is sabotaging your compound."

"I thought you had a line on a merc group," Justine said.

"I did, but when we dug deeper, it turns out the merc group isn't interested in Baron Industries. They were hired to ask some questions and that was it."

"Who would waste money like that?" Justine asked.

"Someone who really hates Nigel."

Nigel rubbed the bridge of his nose. Every time he thought that things couldn't get worse, they did. Now, if Sam was right— and let's face it, Sam wouldn't have called if he'd had any doubts about the veracity of his information—he had an enemy who really hated him.

"Right, but what's the point of threatening Baron Industries here?" Justine asked.

"To lure me here," Nigel said. "Everyone knows I will do anything to keep that plant on schedule. Our entire fiscal year is dependent upon it opening on time."

"Everyone in the business world, or just at Baron?" Sam asked.

"The business world. I gave an interview for *Fortune* magazine, and said that nothing would stop me from reaching our goals. I said that if I had to relocate to Peru and work the factory myself I'd do it."

Silence answered him, and Nigel had a churning in his gut as he realized he might have been responsible for all of this. For the injuries to Paul Masters, for Piper's kidnapping, Jesse's death, Constance . . .

"Have you found out anything about Constance's phone?"

"Yes," Sam said. "Anna is relaying the information to Justine's BlackBerry. I also ran another check on her to make sure we didn't miss anything the first time. She seems clean."

Nigel felt a little better hearing that information. He still couldn't relax, but he did like knowing that the company he'd hired to vet Constance had done a good job.

"If you think of anyone who might have a vendetta against you, let Justine know. I'll be in touch when I have more information."

"Thanks, Sam," Justine said, disconnecting the call. Her phone beeped a second later and she handed it to him.

"Text message from Anna about Constance."

Constance's phone is still sending out a signal that matches Piper's GPS. There's no indication that the phone isn't working. Should we attempt to call? Would you call if you were panicked?

He pulled out his mobile and sent her a quick text message.

Piper okay?

There was no response, but he hoped that she might be able to respond at some time.

"Should we call?" Justine asked.

"Yes," he said. "What if Constance doesn't answer?"

"Then you'll know who your enemy is."

"I wish I knew who we were dealing with," Nigel said.

"Probably a disgruntled employee," she said. "It's definitely someone without the guts to confront you directly."

"That's true," Nigel said, thinking back over the employees they'd let go in the last six months, though no one jumped out at him. He didn't actually fire many of the employees, though he signed all the exit interview materials so that his executives didn't have to deal with any situations like this one.

"I'm going to call Constance," he said, knowing now that her phone was okay.

"Just pretend that you're at the safe house, and want to know what's up with them."

"I will." He dialed Constance's number, and this time the phone rang instead of going to the service interruption message. There was no answer though, and it clicked through to voice-mail. "This is Nigel. We are at the house. Where are you?"

He hung up feeling frustrated and angry. What kind of a man played this type of game? The world was supposed to be civilized, and in a civilized society no one made war on children. And that's exactly what this person was doing.

Nigel couldn't wait to remember a face or a name. He knew that time was running out. "I've got an idea."

"What is it?"

"I'm going to have my VP send me a list of everyone who's been fired in the last year, and then we'll have Anna run a check on them and see if anyone would be behind this."

"Good thinking."

He dialed Derrick's number and the VP answered on the second ring. "It's Nigel."

"I'm glad you called. I had to handle a minor problem this afternoon with some of our middle managers drinking during business lunches."

"Does it need my attention?"

"No, I don't think so. What did you need?"

"Can you compile a list of everyone who's left the company in the last year, and email it to me?"

"I'll get HR to do it. Do you want just those we let go?"

"No. Anyone who has left."

"Is anything wrong?"

"I'm not sure yet. But I need to review the list."

"I'll get it to you first thing tomorrow."

Nigel realized it was after ten. Not that late but certainly not a decent hour. "Sorry for disturbing your evening."

"It's okay. My wife and I were just enjoying a glass of wine."

Nigel hung up a few minutes later. He checked to see if Constance had responded to his text. She hadn't.

"Derrick is going to get the list together in the morning."

"Good. I sent a text to Anna telling her to expect it."

Nigel thought about the people who worked for him. He'd always had a high ranking as a good boss. He demanded a lot from the people who worked for him, but he was fair.

"Could anyone on the board be out to get you?" Justine asked.

"I don't think so. Why?"

"Just that the Barons can't be trusted," Justine said.

"How would you know that?"

Justine couldn't believe she'd said that. "I don't. I'm just tired. Let's see if there is anything on the radio."

She reached for the dial, but Nigel stopped her with his hand on hers. "I don't think so. Explain what you said."

"I didn't mean anything about it. Just that I'd heard that some boards can be cutthroat, and since the company is called Baron Industries and you're not a Baron . . ."

Nigel relaxed his grip on her hand and she put the other one back on the wheel. God, she couldn't believe she said something so stupid. She knew better than to ever comment on anything that the Barons did.

"Well, I don't think our board is like that. A few of the old-timers don't really like having me as the CEO, but they do like the way I've been leading the company, and Derrick—the only other Baron who works on the day-to-day team—isn't really interested in running things."

Derrick. He was Franklin's son. He'd never lived with her and her family. But he'd come to see his dad twice. Once before Franklin had started molesting her, and once afterward, and she'd never really known him.

"Why? Isn't he any good at business?"

"He's okay. But his uncle is always putting him down and saying he's not living up to the Baron name."

Justine didn't think there was anything wrong with that. Living up to the Baron name meant being an uncaring asshole, as far as she was concerned.

"So what do you think about Derrick?"

"I wish he was more decisive, but otherwise he's fine."

"Will he get the list quickly?"

"I think so," Nigel said.

She checked their GPS unit with the map on it, and glanced over at the unit that Nigel was holding. "Are they still moving?"

"No. They stopped."

Justine put on her turn signal and eased the car off the road. She glanced at Nigel's unit so she could check out the address. Piper's signal was still a good four hours ahead of them. But she had the feeling they could make it up if they drove straight through the night.

It took at least a day and a half to get to Cusco. "It's moving again."

"I can see that," Justine said. "We'll just keep going."

"I can drive," Nigel said.

"I can't just ride. I'll make you crazy. I need to do something or I'll go nuts."

She eased back out onto the highway and started driving again. "We should probably plan on stopping for the night."

"I'm not going to be able to sleep while Piper's in danger," Nigel said.

Justine knew he'd change his mind once he saw the way

the highway wound through the mountains. And there were no streetlights like in the States. Despite the fact that they'd made advances in travel in the last few years, the road was still not what they were used to driving on.

"It'll be safer for us if we stop. We'll be more than halfway to Cusco, and I think that's where they are heading."

Justine wasn't going to argue anymore. Nigel wasn't in charge of this operation. "We don't want to be too exhausted when we get to Piper."

He reached over and gripped her right hand hard. "I can't stop while my daughter is still moving. I can't."

"Okay," she said. "We'll keep moving."

There was something in his voice that told her he was serious, and that kind of passion and determination couldn't be stopped. She knew it. She would do her best to keep them both safe as they drove through the night.

"I'm sorry, Justine. I know logically it makes sense to stop, but I just can't do it."

"I wish all parents were like you," she said.

"I think a lot of them are."

"Yes, but not all," Justine said.

"Was your dad like me?"

"Yeah, he was. Man, if anyone had hurt my sister or I while he was alive, he would have gone after them with both barrels blazing."

Nigel let go of her hand, caressing her with his finger before he drew away. "I can understand that. And women are supposed to be fiercer. Was your mom?"

She tried to recall her mother, but to be honest, she had long ago banished the thought of her face from her memory. She and her mom had never been close, and after everything that had happened with Franklin, Justine realized they never would be.

"No. She wasn't into defending anyone."

"What do you mean by that?"

Justine shrugged. This entire situation made it impossible for them not to talk about stuff like parents and parenting, but she didn't want to discuss her own. "Just that my mom thought everyone should defend themselves, and that experience was the best way to learn that lesson."

"Experience is a good teacher," Nigel said.

"Would you really let Piper burn her hand on a hot stove to learn that it's hot?"

"Of course not. Did your mom?"

"Yes."

Justine fumbled in her bag and found her iPod. She jammed the cord that adapted it to play from the radio and turned on her workout mix. It was loud and raucous and exactly what she needed to discourage Nigel from talking anymore.

But the first song to come on was Marvin Gaye's "Sexual Healing." And though the slow melodic song was a favorite of hers for winding down, sitting so close to Nigel and listening to Marvin's smooth voice singing about needing sexual healing made her realize that she needed it, too.

That for a long time there had been an emptiness inside of her that her job just couldn't fill.

And until she'd met Nigel, she'd had no idea what was missing, but having him here with her made everything that had been missing seem very apparent.

She hit the scan button and a new song started to play: "Let's Go," by Trick Daddy. The raucous rap song filled the car and Justine kept her eyes on the road, pretending that Nigel was nothing more than a client.

Chapter Nine

Justine had tuned him out with the loud music, and Nigel really didn't know what to do but to work. Only there was no work to do tonight. So he started thinking of anyone who would have a grudge against him. He was still drawing a blank when his cell phone beeped.

He glanced down to see that he had a text message from Constance.

He opened the message.

Piper fine.

He turned down the music. "Piper's fine. Constance sent a text."

"Good. Check the signal. Are they stopped?"

"No."

"So she must have sent the message when she felt she could do it without being observed."

"I guess," he said.

"What's the matter?"

"I was just thinking about what you'd said earlier . . . I don't think I can trust Constance again. Did Anna figure out where the gunshot came from?"

"I haven't had a message from her, but we could call and check in."

"Do you mind?"

"Not at all." Justine took one hand off the wheel and hit two buttons on her BlackBerry.

"Sterling."

"Nigel wants to know if you have identified who shot Jesse."

"Well . . . I'm not a hundred percent certain, but I'd say the shot came from the backseat. That doesn't mean it was Constance."

"How do you figure?" Nigel asked.

"They could have forced Constance and Piper out of the car," Justine said.

"Exactly. Why?" Anna asked.

"Constance just sent a text saying that Piper was fine."

"She's still moving," Anna said.

Nigel heard the sound of keys being clicked on a keyboard. "I have a lock on her position. Let me see if Sam has any contacts around there. If we can even get someone to drive by or near them to confirm what's going on."

"Sounds great, Anna. I think Sam was already trying that."

"I'll just buzz him and see if we can find anything else. Are you two stopping for the night?"

"No," Nigel said.

"Be careful. The altitude can be dangerous, and your bodies will need time to adjust."

"We're drinking a lot of water," Justine said.

Nigel realized she wasn't going to go back on her word to keep moving. That meant more to him than he would have thought. He liked a lot of things about Justine, but then he'd known that for a while. But now, he was realizing that there was more to her than just the tough-ass bodyguard and that glimpse of a scared woman. There was a deep well of caring, and whether she intended it or not, he felt it directed at him.

"Call us if you find out anything else," Justine said and dis-connected the call.

"Thanks."

"For?"

"Being you."

She gave him a long look. "No one likes me . . . I mean just me. People like things I can do and the fact that I can be counted on . . . but I don't think anyone likes me—

He put a finger over her lips and she turned toward him again.

"I do. I like you a lot."

"Even when I kneed you."

He laughed because he couldn't help himself. "Well, I wasn't thrilled with your actions, but I think you must have had a good reason."

She scratched the back of her neck and watched him with those wide eyes of hers. "I don't know how good the reason is, but I do know that I couldn't help myself."

"Well, then I won't trap you between my body and a wall again."

"Is that all you won't do?" she asked.

She turned her attention back to the road and he could tell she was getting tired. To be honest, he was waning a bit as well, but he was reluctant to stop. Yet at the same time, he didn't want to put Justine in danger.

"I'm still planning to kiss you and hold you. I guess when we make love, you'll have to be on top."

Justine swerved a bit. "Make love? I'm your bodyguard, and that doesn't mean doing anything to your body except keep-ing it alive."

"You talk a lot when you're nervous."

"You are annoying when you talk."

He laughed again and she liked the sound of it. She realized he must be feeling confident they were going to catch up to Piper. Justine knew she'd do anything to make sure they got to her. Protecting the innocent was one of the reasons why she'd originally been drawn to working for Sam.

"So it's annoying that I want to make love to you?"

What was annoying was that he was trying to talk to her about sex. She'd never made love. She'd had sex a few times as an adult . . . well, okay, twice, and it had been nearly unbearable both times. Normally, she didn't like men touching her.

"Stop talking about it."

"Why?"

"Because I said to. I'm not the kind of woman you think I am."

"I think you are supersexy and the most intriguing woman I've ever met."

"Did you think that when I hurt you earlier?"

"Stop using that one reaction as a reason why we can't be together. I made a mistake and pushed one of your buttons. I won't do it again."

"What's to say you won't do it again?" she asked. That was her secret fear. She'd never reacted to any other man the way she reacted to Nigel. He brought out such strong feelings in her that she couldn't always control her reactions. She didn't know what would happen if she tried to actually have sex with Nigel.

Except with him, she didn't think it would be cold and calculated, the way it had been with those two other guys she'd experimented with. With Nigel, she kept telling herself she wasn't going to kiss him again, and yet she was still drawn to him.

"Love, I'm not going to make you any promises other than to say that with me, you don't have to worry about how you react. If you have to knee me again to feel comfortable making love with me, then that's a price I'm willing to pay.

She shook her head. "Why? Are you some kind of masochist?"

"Not at all."

"Then why?"

He shrugged. "You are different to me than other women. I can't explain it better than that. Maybe it's because you connected with Piper, and that I know you'll do whatever it takes to save her. Maybe it's . . . ah, hell, I know what it is. It's you and those hard-as-steel eyes and your curvy body."

"That's lust . . . I can do lust."

"Can you?"

"Hell, I don't know. I hope so. I've never felt this way about any man before. A part of me thinks it's because of how we met. But I'm not sure."

"I'm not sure, either, that I can explain this. It makes no sense . . . the timing is all wrong, but I know that I'm not going to be satisfied until I have you."

"Will you be satisfied once you do? What does that mean?"

"I have no idea . . . I can't promise you forever."

"I don't believe in forever." She could say that honestly. Maybe because of her father dying when she was young, and seeing her mother alone, but Justine had never really thought she'd find a man and spend her entire life with him.

She'd always known she'd move through the world by herself. And looking at Nigel now in the dim light provided by the dashboard, she saw the shadows and planes of his face, and knew she wanted to experience whatever she could with this man.

And since he had an idea that some intimacies made her uncomfortable, she thought she might be able to direct things between them. To keep him in that safety zone where she'd kept the other men she'd had sex with.

"I guess in your line of business, forever isn't something you see a lot of."

"Maybe. But even before working here, I never thought too much of the one-man-one-woman-till-death-do-us-part thing."

"Really? Don't you have any married friends?'

Now probably wasn't a good time to tell him that her friends consisted of Charity and Anna, and that was it. Well, maybe Sam, but she'd never met him face-to-face.

"Charity is in a relationship now."

"Now?"

"She's engaged to Daniel, but in our line of work, it's hard to pull the white-picket-fence routine. It's exciting living on the edge the way we do. Who could give it up to be a stay-at-home wife?"

"Who says you have to?"

Justine didn't answer at first, wanting to make sure she took her time and gave her answer the gravitas it deserved. "Everyone wants that. You know, there's that picture-perfect family in all our heads, and it includes a man, a woman, and a couple of kids. And in most cases, that image is of the man working and the woman taking care of the kids."

Nigel reached over and squeezed her thigh. He kept his big hand there on her leg. His fingers reaching down toward her inner thigh.

"Thats not my image of a perfect family. I'd feel constrained by having to be home every night and by making Piper try to fit in with some PTA-Pleasant-Valley-Sunday kind of place."

"Why are we talking about this? You said sex, not marriage."

"I'm not sure. But I can see we both have ideas about life that don't necessarily mesh."

Justine agreed because she knew Nigel still believed he'd find a woman and fall in love, and she knew absolutely that love of any kind wasn't in the cards for her.

No one could ever love the kind of woman she was. She wasn't cuddly and she wasn't sexy, despite what Nigel had said. And she'd always feel more at home with her Glock in one hand than in a kitchen making cookies. And no matter what Nigel said, a wife had to know how to make cookies.

Nigel like rattling Justine. She seemed so competent and really unaffected by most things that would bother other women.

She was cool in a firefight, hadn't reacted to a dead body, and had been calm when discussing the fact that a nanny might have turned into a kidnapper. But talk to her about making love and she changed. Kiss her and she reacted with passion.

His mobile beeped again and he glanced down to see another text message on his phone from Constance.

I need you, Daddy. Pip.

Nigel almost dropped the phone. "There's a message from Piper on the phone."

"What? What does it say?"

"Just that she needs me."

"Can she give you any other info? Tell her we are coming after her."

<Nigel>: We are coming. Where are you?

<Piper>: Big house. Constance is bleeding and quiet.

<Nigel>: Who hurt her?

<Piper>: The man who took us.

<Nigel>: Are you okay?

<Piper>: Yes. I'm just like Justine. Bye, Daddy.

<Nigel>: Bye, Pip.

Nigel held onto the phone like it was the only link he had to his daughter. He was so glad she was okay. It bothered him that Constance was bleeding and quiet.

"What did Piper say?"

He relayed the text conversation to Justine.

"Do you think Constance is dead?" he asked after a minute.

"I don't know. I doubt he'd bring her all that way to kill her. He probably needs her to watch your daughter. Kidnappers usually either hire someone to watch the kid or drug them."

"Drug them unconscious?" he asked.

"Yes. It's sometimes better because they aren't aware of what's going on. But being drugged like that isn't very good."

"Is this discussion supposed to be helpful?"

"Would you rather I lied?"

"No. Sorry. I just want my little girl."

"I know that, Nigel. I'm doing everything I can to get you to her. This isn't what any of us anticipated."

"I know. I should call my office."

"You might want to wait another couple of hours until they are open."

"I know." The miles continued to go by, and Nigel realized this was the first night he'd spent with a woman in a long time. He'd been too focused on work lately, and maybe that's why he was so attracted to Justine. He had a feeling that if they were in a relationship, she'd demand time with him.

She wouldn't be satisfied with him working all the time . . . he wasn't seriously thinking about a relationship with her, was he? He couldn't be. There was no way he and Justine were going to do anything other than have sex.

"What are you thinking?" she asked.

"About having sex with you."

"Nigel, you need to stop thinking about that."

"Why?"

"Because we can't have sex right now."

"While you're driving?"

"Exactly."

"What if I just reached over there and pleasured you?"

Her hands jerked on the wheel, but she didn't swerve this time. He liked how quick she was. He suspected it was because she was getting used to him and the way he acted around her.

"I'd say you were . . . oh, man, I don't know what I'd do. Why would you want to do that?"

"Because I want to see you come."

He hardened just thinking about it. He did want to see her come. And he wanted to hear the sounds she made as she was turned on. He needed those sounds.

"You do realize you only talk about sex when you are really worried about Piper."

Nigel shook his head. "That's not completely true."

Justine didn't say anything else, and he wondered if she was thinking about him pleasuring her. He was thinking about it. And a part of him wanted to order her to pull over so he could make love to her, but he knew time was of the essence. He'd heard the statistics . . . no, he wasn't going to think about statistics. He was going to concentrate on the fact that Piper was as safe as she could be for the moment, and Justine was here.

Her BlackBerry beeped and she glanced at the screen. Driving while reading text was normally not something he approved of, but Justine did it in a way that was pretty safe. She kept her eyes on the road and read quickly.

"Anna's got someone in the area who is going to the address where Piper is being held."

"Can they take her out of there?"

"I don't know. They wouldn't do it tonight because they need time to check the layout."

"What are you saying? How is this going to help us?"

"We'll have a guy on the inside. That way we can find out who is threatening you and keep Piper safe."

"I want to talk to Anna."

"Why?"

"I think we need to know more about this person she's sending in."

"She doesn't know anything else. Here, read the text."

Justine handed him the phone and he read it again. She'd hired a mercenary to infiltrate the compound. Her guy was to protect Piper and gather information. A part of Nigel applauded the effort, but mainly he just wanted his daughter out of there.

"I'm going to call Sam and tell him to order that guy to get Piper out."

"If he does, Constance will be left for dead, and we may not know who is behind this. Plus, this guy is a merc, Nigel. Do you know what that means?"

"I know that he works for Liberty Investigations."

"He's a gun for hire, and we don't know how good he is with kids."

"Piper isn't like other kids," Nigel said.

He had placed his trust in Liberty Investigations, and even though the car they'd hired had been sabotaged, he wasn't going to change his mind now. He knew they were doing their level best to get Piper back.

And he was doing the same.

"What else can we do?"

"At this point, nothing. If you are the praying kind of guy, then I'd do that."

He had already prayed for God to watch over his daughter.

"Are you the praying kind?"

She looked over at him with those serious wide eyes of hers. "I never really have been."

"Why not?"

She shrugged. "I always thought if there was really someone up there, he would watch over those who couldn't protect themselves, and keep them safe. Yet the innocent still keep being hurt . . . "

"So therefore, there isn't a God?"

"Something like that," she said, turning away and ending the conversation.

Nigel realized then that someone or something had harmed Justine's innocence, and that person or incident had shaped her into the woman she was today.

Chapter Ten

They had to stop for gas just before dawn. Anna's contact hadn't sent any messages, and that was more frustration than Justine had ever experienced before, waiting to hear from the contact about Piper.

She'd seen Nigel reread the text message conversation he'd had with his daughter a bunch of times, but she knew it wasn't enough. She'd been teasing him when she'd said that he only talked about sex when he was worried about Piper, but she did realize he needed the distraction.

And she needed it, too. They were about to explode from exhaustion and tension.

"Is there a shower we can use?" she asked the attendant in Spanish.

"Upstairs. You have to pay for the water and the room."

"No problem," she said. She paid the man and then turned to Nigel.

"Why are we showering? I need to get the grime off me. We've had a long night and this will refresh me. Do you want a shower?"

"With you?"

"No. But you can go first if you want."

"That wouldn't be gentlemanly."

"I'm not one to stand on ceremony."

"I am."

Another thing they didn't have in common. She didn't need proof they were different. She knew they were. But there was this small part of her that kind of hoped they weren't. That there would be some kind of magical thing that would change all that.

He looked back at the attendant and asked if he had any clothes they could buy. The man pointed to a rack filled with T-shirts that advertised the city they were in, and wildly colored skirts. Nigel paid for two T-shirts, and they followed the man upstairs to what appeared to be his private apartment.

"You take time," he said in broken English before he left.

Nigel looked around the sparsely furnished room. "Humble."

"Very humble," Justine agreed, but she didn't care. Trappings didn't matter too much to her. They never had. She knew that safety and contentment came from inside her, not from the things that were around her.

"Go ahead and shower," he said.

"Um . . . don't take this the wrong way, but I'd feel better if you were in there with me."

"Now you're talking."

"Not for sex. Just so I can make sure you're safe."

Justine didn't want to think about getting naked while Nigel was in the same room with her. The two sexual encounters she'd had as an adult had involved very little nudity, mainly just clothing pushed out of the way for the sake of intercourse.

"Lead the way," he said.

She walked into the bathroom and checked out the small claw-foot tub. There was a small spigot suspended over the tub. It was primitive, but it would get them clean, and that was all that mattered. She put the lid down on the toilet seat and gestured to Nigel.

"There. Now you can be comfortable."

She checked out the window and then locked the door. "Do you still have your gun?"

"Yes. Am I going to need it?"

"I hope not, but you should get it out in case you do. I have the Glock with me and a little Beretta. Do you want one of them?"

"No. I have my gun right here. I will keep us safe while you shower," he said.

Those were words she'd never heard before. No one had ever kept her safe. She guarded everyone in her life. "I . . . okay."

She took off her boots and socks, and then climbed into the tub, preparing to draw the shower curtain.

"Don't."

She hesitated. "What do you want?"

"Get undressed out here. Let me see you, love."

She hesitated, as this was what she was afraid of. She didn't know if she could do it. The longer she hesitated, the more nervous she got, and finally she just shook her head. "I don't think I can."

He stood up and came closer, but didn't crowd her. The tub was behind her and there was plenty of space all around them.

"I want to see your body, Justine. Don't you want me to see your body?"

She did and she didn't. She was so unsure of herself, she wanted to say screw it and just grab the guns and leave.

"I'd rather see your body," she said at last. She'd wanted something to happen between them and she'd never been a coward. Was she seriously going to start being one now?

"Fair enough," he said. Stepping back, he unbuttoned his shirt and shrugged out of it. He dropped it on the floor at her feet. He had on T-shirt underneath his Kevlar vest. And she could see the muscles of his arms and chest defined by the cotton shirt.

"Your turn now."

She reached for the hem of her T-shirt, and even knowing that her entire torso was covered in Kevlar, she still hesitated.

Nigel leaned over and brushed his lips over hers, soft and gentle. "You don't have to."

She put her hands on his face, staring up into his eyes, and realized she wanted to. She kissed him with all the passion she'd been trying to pretend she didn't feel. Then stepped back and drew her shirt up and over her head.

Nigel skimmed his gaze over her curvy body. The black Kevlar vest against her pale skin was a nice contrast. And it fit her perfectly. She wrapped one arm around her waist, keeping her eyes on his chest.

"Okay, take off your vest."

"Only if you kiss me first," he said. He had the feeling this was going to be the only chance he had to make love to Justine, and he wasn't about to waste it.

She shook her head. "You have to kiss me."

He leaned over, careful to keep distance between their bodies. The room was light and he made sure that he didn't crowd her. But he didn't keep his kiss light. He thrust his tongue deep into her mouth, tasting her as deeply as he could. He ran his fingers over the edge of the vest, tracing a path between her soft skin and the tough Kevlar. He found the Velcro fastenings and undid them while his mouth was on hers.

He wanted her completely naked, and he wanted her that way right now. He finally got the vest loosened and drew it off her body, stepping back and letting the kiss end between them.

He caught her wrists before she could draw her arms over her chest again. She wore a plain cotton bra under the vest and her breasts were full—bigger than he'd expected. Her nipple was beaded against the fabric of the bra.

He reached out and lightly stroked her nipple with his fingertip. She shivered and shifted her shoulders.

"Kiss me again, Nigel."

His name on her lips was like an aphrodisiac. It went straight to his groin, hardening him and making him impatient with the slow seduction he was trying to give her.

He brought her closer to him, wrapping one arm around her waist. "Okay?"

"Yes," she said, leaning up on tiptoe and drawing his mouth down to hers. She rubbed her lips back and forth over his, then traced over the seam of his lips with her tongue. He opened his mouth to breathe and got a taste of her breath, and then her sweet tongue.

He felt her hands moving over him, unfastening the vest and removing it with a surety he knew he didn't have. Then her hands slid under his T-shirt, and he was the one shuddering at the feel of her hands on his naked flesh. Her touch was electric and drove away thoughts of anything except Justine.

He caressed her back and the fragile curve of her spine, running his hands further down her back and cupping her ass, drawing her closer to him. He rubbed the tip of his erection against the junction of her thighs. She moaned and wrapped one leg around his waist, trying to lift herself onto his body.

He unfastened her bra, pulling back to draw it off her body. God, she was exquisitely made. But as he looked closer, he saw scars on her torso. There were two bullet wounds. One under her ribs, and another right above her spleen.

She had a knife wound on her one of her breasts, and a long scar that ran from under her arm around to her back.

"Sorry I'm so ugly."

He shook his head. She wasn't ugly. He lowered his head and traced all the scars on her body with his tongue. Worshipped those wounds she'd gathered in her life. This body was the epitome of what she was. It showed Justine as she really was. Sexy and sure and confident and wounded. A wounded warrior that he wanted to worship.

Her skin prickled under his touch, and she moaned when he got to the knife wound at her breast. He hesitated, letting his breath caress her first. She put her hands in his hair and shifted her body so that her nipple brushed his lips. He rubbed them back and forth over her distended flesh, enjoying the feel of her. He touched his tongue to her nipple and she moaned.

"Okay, love?"

"Yes," she said her voice low and breathy. "But I need more."

"I'm not done," he said, before sucking her nipple into his mouth. He held it lightly with his teeth and suckled her. He felt her shifting against him as he sucked strongly on her flesh. He reached for her other breast, the one unmarred by scars, and caressed that nipple with his thumb and forefinger.

Her body arched in his arms, and he felt her hands on his head, trying to draw him away from her breasts. But he wasn't done yet. He hadn't tasted his fill of her breasts or her body. He wanted to stretch her out on a bed and spend hours just exploring her. But there wasn't time for that. There was just this small bathroom with the naked lightbulb.

He kissed his way up her body from her breasts to her sternum, and then to the base of her neck, biting her lightly and sucking on the flesh. She clutched at him again. Said his name in that breathy voice one more time before he captured her lips with his and took complete control of her. He cupped her ass and drew her closer to him. Let her rock her center over his cock. He rotated his hips until he heard her moan really deep in her throat and felt her fingernails dig into his shoulders.

He knew she was on the edge of a powerful orgasm by the way she was breathing and moaning and arching toward him. He slipped one hand between their bodies, but was frustrated to find a thick belt. He couldn't undo it one-handed, so had to settle for caressing her through her pants.

He traced a path over her zipper and knew he'd found the right spot when she grabbed his wrist and held his hand to her body. Her hips were rocking against him and she wrenched her mouth from his to cry out his name, to moan it loudly and with such passion that he knew he'd never forget it, never forget this moment in this bathroom in a small town in Peru.

His world was falling apart around him, but he'd found himself in her arms.

Justine had never experienced an orgasm before with anyone else in the room. And as Nigel held her and drew out her orgasm, she wanted to scream. She was pretty sure she might have.

She finally figured out what emotional connections were all about, because in this moment, she felt closer to Nigel then she'd ever felt to any other person. It was almost like that moment when they'd been attacked at the airport and they'd fought side by side.

She stopped shaking and felt so incredibly alive in that moment. She liked the feel of Nigel's chest against her bare breasts. Her nipples were still hard and sensitive and as she brushed them against his warm skin, she realized she wasn't ready for all this touching between them to stop.

"That was nice," she said, quietly.

"I'm glad you liked it," he said, tucking a strand of her hair behind her ear. "Any bad moments?"

She shook her head.

"Good. How do you feel about doing some more touching, and maybe losing those trousers?"

"I . . ."

He leaned down and kissed her so softly and so gently. "If you want to stop now, we can."

"I'm not sure that I want that."

"Then, why don't you take off that belt?"

She looked down at the belt and realized he hadn't unzipped her pants. She couldn't believe she'd come that hard from him just touching her breasts and between her legs.

She looked over at him and found he was staring at her breasts. "You have an incredibly sexy body."

"Even with the scars?"

"Hell, yes. Everything about you turns me on."

She blushed and turned away, unfastening her belt and drawing it through the belt loops. She dropped it onto the floor and turned back to him.

Nigel had finished stripping. His body was incredible. He was solid muscle from his neck to his toes. She slowly let her gaze drift down his body. His cock was hard and strong, sticking out from his body. She reached out to touch him, starting at his neck and running her fingers over his chest. She took her time caressing his pecs and then moved lower. He had a wound on his left side. A knife wound that looked like someone had been aiming for his heart but had been knocked off target at the last second. She remembered the feel of his lips on her scars and leaned down to trace the scar with her tongue. His hands came up to her hair, resting lightly against the back of her head as she kissed the length of that scar.

His skin tasted faintly salty but smelled delicious. She had never really had the chance to explore a man's body before. She wanted to take her time, but she knew this wasn't the right moment for it. Yet she couldn't rush. She took her time touching him. Experiencing the different textures of his body. The softness of his skin, the hard strength of the muscles underneath, and the springiness of the hair curling on his chest.

"I need you, love," he said.

She looked up at his serious eyes. His erection brushed her stomach as she wrapped her arms around his body and drew them together. His skin was both warm and cool from the breeze in the room. He wrapped his arms around her and tucked his chin on the top of her head. She was completely touching him, skin to skin, and she wanted more. She needed more.

She had no idea what to do. All of her sexual encounters had taken place with her lying on her back. As she glanced around the small bathroom, she knew there was no place for that type of lovemaking.

"I want you, Nigel."

"Good." He bent again to kiss her and started building the passion inside her once again. His hands were on her breasts, pulling at her nipples and making her squirm, as moisture pooled between her legs. He skimmed his hands down her back and drew her up on her tiptoes. He lifted her up.

"Wrap your legs around my waist," he said.

She did and he turned and leaned back against the bathroom wall. "Put me inside you, love. Take me."

Justine hesitated and then shifted on his cock until he was positioned at the portal of her body. He was big and as she tried to lower herself on him, she couldn't get him inside.

She shifted again, determined to take him. She felt Nigel's hands on her butt, holding her, and then reaching lower to part her body around his cock. He slipped inside her body and she shifted on him, then he slid deep inside her.

"You feel so good," he said, his words a hoarse whisper in her ear.

She thought so, too. She'd never really enjoyed having a man in her body before this. He kissed her neck, biting gently, and then whispered for her to move.

She shifted on him, pulling up until only the tip of his cock remained inside of her, and then she brought her body down on him, until he was once again deeply seated inside of her.

She moved against him, varying her rhythm until she found one that allowed her to grind her clit against him when he thrust up inside of her.

The motion felt so incredibly good that she came almost at once, but he gripped her waist and called her name.

"Come with me this time."

She didn't know if she could. "I'm going to come, Nigel. Any second now."

He nodded and clutched her buttocks in his hands. He took control of her motions, rocking her body up and down on his cock. He kissed her hard until she was completely surrounded by him. Overwhelmed by the feel of his mouth on hers, his body inside hers, his breath in her ear.

"Now, love. Now."

She looked into those serious eyes of his and came when he commanded it. Pleasure rippled out from her center, and she felt like she was reborn in his arms.

She held on tightly to him until she realized what she was doing, and what exactly she was feeling. She couldn't need Nigel Carter. She wasn't going to allow that to happen.

But as she closed her eyes and inhaled deeply, the scent of his body surrounding her, she wanted nothing more than to cling tightly to him.

To hold on as tightly as she could to those big shoulders of his, and rest her head right over his heart.

Hell, no, she thought. She wasn't falling for Nigel. Not after the rough time she'd given Charity for falling in love with the wrong man at the wrong time.

She couldn't possibly be making the same mistake Charity had. But Justine knew she wasn't. She was nothing like the former supermodel.

And Nigel was nothing like Daniel. He wasn't lying to her

to protect her. He was simply holding her and making love to her, probably to distract himself from the fact that his daughter was missing.

She understood that and leaned down to drop a soft kiss on his shoulder and ran her finger over the bandage there. One she hoped he didn't even feel, because that kiss was for her. That kiss was her way of thanking him for making her feel like the woman she always wanted to be.

Chapter Eleven

Nigel separated his body from Justine's and realized he'd come inside her without giving a thought to birth control. Watching the way Justine turned on the shower and kept her back to him, he guessed now wasn't the time to bring up the subject. He went to the sink to wash his penis, and when he heard her step into the shower, turned to join her.

He saw tears in her eyes and they were so out of character for her, he was alarmed.

"Justine?"

"Don't say anything," she said, her voice low.

"What's the matter? Oh, fuck, did I hurt you?"

"No, you didn't hurt me."

"Then, what is it?"

"I said I don't want to talk. Let's shower and get back on the road."

There had been many times in Nigel's life when he'd slept with a woman and walked out the door as quickly as he fallen into her arms, but he'd never suspected it felt like this. He wanted to draw her back into his arms and cuddle her close. He wanted to spend five minutes enjoying the aftermath of their lovemaking, and instead, she was rushing him.

"Move over, then," he said. "We've wasted enough time."

She didn't say anything else as they both washed, climbed out of the shower, and dried off. She got dressed, reminding him to put on his Kevlar vest. Then she changed the bandage from his earlier gunshot wound.

"Thank you, Nigel."

"For what?"

"For that. I've never really enjoyed sex before. . . . I didn't know it could be like that."

"You don't have to thank me for that. It was my pleasure."

"I'm not dealing well with everything. I'm not used to taking care of anyone but me away from the job . . . I'm making a hash of this."

"It's okay. I think I know what you mean."

She shook her head. "Then explain it to me, because I don't understand it."

"You're a loner, and you just realized you like having someone else in your life."

Nigel finished getting dressed and tucked his gun into the holster at the small of his back. He noticed that Justine had done the same. She checked out the window. The first rays of dawn were breaking over the horizon.

He watched the woman he made love to disappear as the bodyguard came back to the fore. She was professional and quiet as she opened the bathroom door and scanned the room. She swept her gun from left to right, then signaled him to follow her.

They made their way downstairs, thanking the attendant for the shower. The Humvee was where they left it. Nigel opened the passenger side door, and since Justine was right beside him, he caught her around the waist and lifted her inside.

"I'm driving."

"I thought—"

"You thought wrong. I'm going to be driving from here on out. You can read and text and protect us with your gun."

"Nigel, you can't tell me what to do just because we had sex."

"I had already decided to drive. Don't waste your breath. I'm not changing my mind."

He got behind the wheel and was glad when she didn't argue any more. They were finally on their way, and he realized Justine was the woman he'd spent the most amount of time with in a long time. And he didn't mind it. Normally he needed space, but not with her.

"What are you thinking?" she asked.

"About calling my office," he said, pulling his mobile phone from the dash where he'd left it.

"Good idea. I'm going to check in with Anna and Charity, and see what they've uncovered."

Nigel called his office to see if they'd received any further threats, but his administrative assistant didn't have any messages for him. She did have a document from HR that had a list of all the people who'd left the company in the last year.

He was impressed with how quickly Derrick had gotten the information together, and dictated a thank-you memo to him via his secretary.

He hung up the phone.

"Well?" Justine said.

"Derrick got the list together and my assistant is emailing it. We should have it shortly."

"Good. Anna hasn't found anything more on any of your employees, but she did determine that the car that forced Jesse off the road was a large truck. She is running it through her database to see who uses that type of vehicle in this country.

"Charity is on her way to your factory just in case whoever has Piper shows up there with a threat. There wasn't anything delivered to the house you were supposed to stay at last night."

"I'll call my office here."

"Good idea."

Nigel had to call his office back in the States in order to get the number for the Cusco office. He was patched through, and Alfred Tamlin, who was the security officer in charge, was very glad to hear from him. There had been a package dropped off for him just before dawn.

"What's in the package, Alfred?"

"I haven't opened it."

"You may do so now," Nigel said, covering the mouthpiece and turning to Justine. "I'm going to put this on speaker."

He activated the speakerphone.

"It's a letter, sir. It says . . . you have twenty-four hours to bring two million dollars to the ruins if you want to see your daughter and her nanny alive."

Justine wasn't surprised by the threat, and from the look on Nigel's face, he wasn't either.

"Is there a signature or a name?"

"No, sir, I don't think so . . . wait a minute. Just some initials, J.E.B."

"Alfred, this is Justine O'Neill from Liberty Investigations. Do you have a fax machine?"

"Yes ma'am."

"Good. Will you please send a fax to this number?" Justine gave Alfred Anna's mobile fax number. She could receive faxes anywhere in the world from that number.

"Sir, is that okay?"

"Yes, Alfred. Let me know if anything else arrives. Here is my mobile number."

Nigel hung up once he'd given the man his number.

"Do those initials mean anything to you?" Justine asked.

"Not off the top of my head. I'm going to call back my assistant and have her check for any names on the list."

"Check your email first. The fewer people we involve in this the better."

"Here, you check while I drive," he said, handing her his smart phone. She accessed his email program and saw that the list had arrived. She forwarded a copy to Anna and then opened it up.

She scanned it, looking for the initials, but they weren't on there. "No one jumps out as having those initials."

"Is Piper's GPS signal still stationary?"

Justine checked it. "Yes, it is."

"Well, that's one good thing," he said.

"All of this is good, Nigel. The kidnapper has made contact and demanded money. We know what he wants and where he's going to be. Do you have two million? Do you want to pay the ransom?"

"I have the money and I'd pay anything to get Piper back, but I don't want to leave her a target for kidnappers."

"Okay. We will get her back without paying if we can; I just had to know if you'd be able to pay. What would you do to raise the money?"

"I'd have the money wired from my account in Switzerland to a bank here in Cusco."

"I think you should do that so he thinks you are following his orders. I'm going to ask Anna to drive with someone who looks similar to you from the safe house to Cusco. If they leave now and the kidnapper has someone watching the house, he'll believe you are following orders."

Justine knew she was dumping a lot on Nigel, but she felt like talking this way was the best thing for him, particularly after hearing that death threat to Piper. And Justine couldn't handle anything sexual right now. She was dealing with some odd feelings from their lovemaking. There was the pleasure he'd given her, which had been nice, but she had wanted to stay in his arms.

She'd wanted to rest against him, which wasn't like her at all. It was like one moment in his arms, and she forgot that she couldn't rely on any man. She could only trust herself.

"What else do we need to do?"

"That's it for now. I'll take care of those details. You just drive."

"I'm glad I'm behind the wheel," he said.

"Why?"

"Otherwise I think I'd lose it. I can't believe this kidnapper threatened her life."

Justine reached over and patted Nigel's thigh. He glanced at her hand for a second, and then brought his down on top of it. He joined their fingers together.

"I'm so glad I hired your company."

"Me, too," she said, meaning it. She had thought working for Baron Industries was going to be a nightmare, but meeting Nigel was actually helping her put to rest some nightmares from her past that she'd never been able to lose before.

She squeezed his fingers before letting go of his hand. She started sending messages off on her mobile phone to both Anna and Charity. She ended up talking to Anna on the phone.

"Have you heard from your contact inside?" Justine asked.

"Yes. He's seen the girl and she's well. Unharmed, and being kept in a nice room. The nanny, Constance, has a minor injury, and she was treated for it. They are keeping them both in separate rooms for right now."

"When will he check in again?" Justine asked.

"In three hours."

"We won't be in Cusco then, but we should be there by early afternoon. Can he meet up with me in the city somewhere to give me the layout of the buildings, and all that?"

"I'll set something up. How's the drive?"

"Not bad. The road is pretty nice, it's just the terrain that's slowing us down."

"Good. How's Nigel?"

"Fine."

"How are you?"

"Uh, fine. Why are you asking all these questions?"

"Because you were weird at the airport when I came outside. What was going on with you?"

"Nothing. I just needed a minute. I'm fine now."

"You know there's no shame in admitting you need to talk," Anna said.

"I don't need to talk. Everything's fine. Call me when you have my meeting set up with your guy."

She hung up without saying good-bye. She knew Anna meant well and had only been trying to be a supportive friend, but the last thing she wanted to do was talk about personal stuff.

Especially personal stuff about Nigel when he was sitting right next to her.

"You okay?"

"Yes. Sorry about that. Anna is going to set up a meeting with her guy on the inside for me. I think if we know the layout, we'll be able to go in there and get Piper and Constance out."

Nigel could tell something was bothering Justine by the way she kept fidgeting in her seat. She'd cleaned and checked the ammo on every weapon in the Humvee, and kept checking her mobile phone.

"What's the matter?"

"Nothing," she said. "I'm not really in the mood to talk."

He wasn't, either, but he was tired of the scenarios in his head that involved Piper and Constance. "Have you ever made love like that before?"

"No," she said. "I'm not big into sex."

"I'm not either, but I've made love in different positions."

"Well, until you, I was a missionary-position person."

"Really?" he asked. "Why?"

Nigel saw her hesitate and he knew she was contemplating telling him to mind his own damn business. Which would be understandable, but he needed the distraction and he wanted to know everything there was to know about Justine.

"I just didn't like it."

"Like sex? I would think that the missionary position wouldn't work for you since you don't like a guy crowding you."

"I don't like it. But I was trying to get over my fears when I experimented with sex."

"When was that?"

"About ten years ago."

"You were quite young to be afraid of sex and men," Nigel said.

"Yeah, I was. Don't ask me anything else, Nigel. I'd have to lie to you and I don't want to"

He nodded. "I guess that's fair. But you know, some things, when you hold onto them, just grow bigger over time."

"This one can't get any bigger than it is."

"I'm not sure about that. Like right now in my head, I'm thinking of all the horrible things that could happen to Piper while the kidnapper has her, but talking to you is alleviating that."

Justine saw his point, but there was no way she was telling him about her past. There were only two people alive who know who Justine O'Neill used to be, and that was one too many as far as Justine was concerned.

"I'm glad that talking to me is helping you. We're not going to let any of those bad things happen to Piper. I promise."

"Don't make promises you can't keep," Nigel said.

"I'm not. We have a jump on this guy thanks to your secret GPS, and that's all we need."

"I never thought that bunny would save her life."

"It's always the things that seem like the little pieces that end up saving the day," Justine said.

"Really?"

"Yes," she said, and told him stories from past jobs where it seemed like they were up against big odds and still they were able to save their client.

"Liberty Investigations doesn't lose. We aren't going to let anything happen to Piper. And we'll find out how the kidnapper knew where Jesse was going, and fix that leak as well."

"The leak might be on my side," Nigel said.

"That's true. Your office knew where you were flying to and when you'd be arriving. We will keep looking into it. Does J.E.B. mean anything to you? Not a name, but a project, or anything?"

Nigel didn't say anything, but kept driving. She could tell his focus had turned inward. And she let him think about the question she'd asked. Figuring out who the kidnapper was would give them a big leg up in their investigation.

But even without that information, Justine knew they'd get Piper back alive. The same way she'd known Franklin would go after Millie the night he had . . . the night she'd finally killed him. She had an instinct when it came to kids and crimes. She always had.

"I can't recall anything," Nigel said after a few moments.

"I wonder if the initials aren't meant to be a word," she said. "Does JEB mean anything to you? Do you know anyone with that nickname?"

"No, I don't," he said, then pulled his hands off the wheel and slammed them down again. "Dammit. I can't think of anything. The harder I concentrate, the more blanks I draw."

She suspected he was tired and running on adrenaline right now. She certainly was. It had been a long twenty-four hours, and while she'd been on jobs like this one in the past, she couldn't recall one that was so draining on her emotions. She could handle the physical stress—she worked out so that her body was in tip-top shape—but this emotional crap was killing her.

And she wasn't even Piper's parent or relative. She had only met the girl a few short hours ago. What must Nigel be going through?

"Why don't you let me drive for a while?"

"No. I can't sit there again. It was making me crazy."

She nodded. It was making her crazy to sit here and wait for something to happen. For a break to come in their investigation that would unlock the puzzle of what was going on in Peru. It was clear that someone was out to get Nigel. But a part of Justine wondered if it was personal or business. Was Baron Industries the real target, or was it Nigel Carter?

Driving to Cusco was really all they could do, but it didn't make the trip any easier on either one of them.

"What is the new compound here called?" Justine asked, trying to ask questions that would jar something in Nigel, and make the initials at the bottom of that ransom note mean something.

"The Cusco factory," he said. "Believe me, I've thought of every possible angle on those initials. It's just not anything obvious."

"It has to be something you'd know," she said. "This person took your daughter, Nigel. He wants you to suffer, and he wants you to know he was the one who did it."

"Then why doesn't he just get on the phone and call me?"

"Don't be sarcastic. I'm just pointing out that you probably know what those initials stand for."

He scrubbed a hand through his hair. "I know, I just can't think of what it means. And I'm tired, Justine. And worried about my little girl."

She reached over and put her hand on his thigh, squeezing him. "I'm here with you, and together we will figure this out."

"What makes you so sure?"

She shrugged. She'd already given him all the verbal reassurance she could. He had to decide if he was going to believe
Piper would be okay or if he was going to continue to worry
over her. There was nothing Justine could say to change his
mind, and she knew that.

But a part of her believed that if he were the man she was
coming to know him to be, that he would let his fear fall away.
Because until he did, he wasn't going to be able to see anything but his fear for his daughter, and Justine knew that wasn't
going to make it easier for them to find her.

Chapter Twelve

They arrived in Cusco in the middle of the afternoon. Nigel followed her directions to the house that Liberty Investigations had rented. They parked the car and immediately went to their computers, both of them downloading emails and information. Anna had designed a computer program to run combinations of words based on a set of variables, all creating the initials J.E.B.

Nigel was going through the list while Justine walked around the plush house. They were at a high altitude, and the beauty that was the Amazon Basin surrounded her, but Justine felt restless. She had to meet Anna's contact in less than an hour.

She was still trying to decide the best way to disguise Nigel. She had hoped to leave him at the house, but he refused to stay, and she was still his bodyguard, so she couldn't take a chance with his life.

She had some spray-on hair dye that would change the color of his hair, and clothes that would definitely change his image.

"Justine?"

"Yes?"

"Are you ready to go?"

"I will be as soon as we get you in disguise."

He entered the living room and she was surprised to see he'd already used the hair dye. He looked different to her, with the deep red hair and the garb that college students tended to wear. Faded and worn jeans, a tight T-shirt, and a scruffy-looking hat.

"What do you think?"

"Pretty good. Let's go. I want some time to get you in position so I can keep you safe."

"I'm almost ready," he said.

He crossed to her and drew her in to his arms, kissing her deeply before letting her go. "Sorry about that, but I missed the taste of you."

He walked away before she could react. All she could do was follow him out the door to the car. Nigel was entirely too confident in himself sexually, and he wasn't afraid to use that masculine confidence against her. He was making her feel like she was very desirable.

And she didn't mind it as much as she thought she would have. There was something about the way Nigel looked at her that put her fears from the past to rest. She knew that was dangerous because it made her depend too much on him, but on the other hand, having Nigel in her life was something she realized she really wouldn't mind.

She drove through the streets of Cusco on a motorcycle. Nigel straddled the seat behind her. She liked the feel of him pressed against her, and didn't feel trapped by him at all.

He caressed her breasts as she drove and she found that she liked it. When they stopped and he helped her off the bike, she missed the feel of his hands on her breasts. She couldn't wait to make love with him again. But she had no idea if they would have the time.

It was the first time her desires as a woman got in the way of her instincts as a professional bodyguard.

Nigel linked their fingers together as they walked back through town to the outdoor café where Justine was to meet her contact. She found a table for her and Nigel near the café wall. With the wall at their backs, they only had three sides to defend. They ordered Dos Equis and sat in the sun to wait. She felt sweat bead up between her breasts and slowly slide down her skin.

Nigel leaned over to her and licked a drop of sweat from her neck. "God, woman, you are so hot."

"Literally," she said, not really sure how to take all the sexual compliments he continued to give her.

"Me, too. After we take care of business here, I'm going to make love to you."

She shivered. "Really?"

He smiled at her so sweetly she knew she was falling for him. He leaned forward and kissed her. "Yes."

A bus rumbled by and less than a minute later, a man who looked as if he'd seen the inside of more than one prison ambled toward them. Justine dropped Nigel's hand and pulled her gun under the table, prepared to shoot their way out of the café if they had to.

"This seat taken?" the guy asked.

"No," Justine answered.

"I'm Emile," he said.

"Justine."

"Do you have the money?" he asked.

Justine nodded and Nigel passed him an envelope under the table. He pocketed it without opening it. "I've drawn a basic layout for you, and I think tonight might be the time to make your move. I can meet you inside the south wall at eight."

He left a small paper on the table before getting up and leaving. Justine drew the paper toward her and examined it. The diagram of the complex was very detailed, and the notes on the side giving them directions to the location were done in very neat handwriting.

"Can we trust him?" Nigel asked.

"As far as you can trust anyone you pay."

Nigel gave her a hard stare as they stood up and left the café. "What does that mean?"

"Just that as long as you are the highest bidder, you're the one who owns the man—if you call that loyalty."

"So how do you know if you're the high man?"

Justine climbed on the motorcycle and waited for Nigel to climb on behind her. "You don't, until you're too deep to turn around."

"Nice," he said.

She turned on the engine and gunned the motor, shooting them down the street. She didn't head immediately back to the house they were renting, just in case anyone had followed them. When she was sure they weren't being followed, she returned to the house and pulled into the garage. Nigel got off the bike first, and when she stepped off, he drew her into his arms and kissed her.

Nigel loved riding through the streets of Cusco with Justine. It made him feel like he was really alive, something he thought he'd never feel again when Piper was taken.

But more than that, it helped take his mind off the horrible images that had plagued him the car. Thinking about Piper wasn't helping anyone. He was doing everything in his power to save his daughter, and now all he could do was wait.

Waiting was hard, but the man who'd brought them the diagram looked capable, and Nigel believed he'd protect his daughter.

And right now he had this woman in his arms. A woman he'd been thinking about in inconvenient sexual terms since he'd met her. She pulled away from him and walked into the house. He stood there for a moment watching her.

She moved like she had earlier this evening in the lobby, all easy, long-limbed grace. Each step was slowly measured. Her shoulders were back and her hips moved sensuously.

"Do you want me, Justine?" he asked her.

"Yes. I do. I'm not sure what to do about it."

"Let's go inside and I'll show you."

He took her hand and led her into the house. It was cool after the heat of the city. He knew not to lead her into the bedroom. She wasn't comfortable enough with him yet to make love to him in a bed, and he knew that.

Instead, he sat down on the long couch and drew her down next to him, onto his lap. She turned around until she straddled his lap.

"Comfortable?"

"Yes." She pushed back from him, putting one hand between them. "Nigel?"

"Yes?"

"How about taking off your shirt?" Justine asked.

He arched one eyebrow at her. "Do you have something in mind?"

"Yes. Can I . . . I mean, would you just sit here and let me . . ."

He growled deep in her throat when she leaned forward to brush kisses against his chest. Her lips were sweet and not shy as she explored his torso. Then he felt the edge of her teeth as she nibbled at his pecs.

He watched her, his eyes narrowing and his pants feeling damned uncomfortable. Her tongue darted out and brushed against his nipple. He arched off the couch, and put his hand on the back of her head, urging her to stay where she was.

She put her hands on his shoulders and eased her way down his chest. She traced each of the muscles that ribbed his abdomen and then slowly made her way lower. He could feel his heartbeat in his erection, and knew he was going to lose it if he didn't take control.

But another part of him wanted to just sit back and let her

have her way with him. When she reached the edge of his pants, she stopped and glanced up his body to his face.

Her hand going to his erection, brushing over his straining length. "I guess you like that."

"Hell, yeah," he said, pulling her to him. He lifted her slightly so that her nipples brushed his chest.

"Now it's my turn," he said.

She nibbled on her lips as he rotated his shoulders so that his chest rubbed against her breast.

"I like that," she said.

Blood roared in his ear. He was so hard, so full right now, that he needed to be inside her body.

Impatient with the fabric of her clothing, he shoved her shirt out of his way and undid her pants. "Stand up and take those pants off."

She did as he asked and he shed his pants at the same time, making sure to grab the condom he'd put in his pocket.

He pulled her back onto his lap and caressed her creamy thighs. God, she was soft. She moaned as he neared her center and then sighed when he brushed his fingertips across the crotch of her panties.

The cotton was warm and wet. He slipped one finger under the material and hesitated for a second, looking down into her eyes.

Her eyes were heavy-lidded. She bit down on her lower lip, and he felt the minute movements of her hips as she tried to move his touch where she needed it.

He was beyond teasing her or prolonging anything. He ripped her panties aside, plunging two fingers into her humid body. She squirmed against him.

He pulled her head down to his so he could taste her mouth. Her mouth opened over his and he told himself to take it slow, but slow wasn't in his programming with this woman. She was pure feminine temptation and he had her in his arms.

He nibbled on her and held her at his mercy. Her nails dug into his shoulders and she leaned up, brushing against his chest. Her nipples were hard points and he pulled away from her mouth, glancing down to see them pushing against his chest.

He caressed her back and spine, scraping his nail down the length of it. He followed the line of her back down to the indentation above her backside.

She closed her eyes and held her breath as he fondled her, running his finger over her nipple. It was velvety compared to the satin smoothness of her breast. He brushed his finger back and forth until she bit her lower lip and shifted on his lap. He wanted to give her this pleasure because from the few things she'd said, he guessed that her experiences with men hadn't been that great, in bed or out.

He saw the sexy confident woman she was disappear each time he pulled her into his arms. He wanted to know who had harmed this woman, so he could exact vengeance on them. He needed to wrap her in his arms and keep her safe for the rest of both of their days.

She moaned a sweet sound that he leaned up to capture in her mouth. She tipped her head to the side, immediately allowing him access to her mouth. She held his shoulders and moved on him, rubbing her center over his erection.

He scraped his fingernail over her nipple and she shivered in his arms. He pushed her back a little bit so he could see her. Her breasts were bare, nipples distended and begging for his mouth. He lowered his head and suckled.

He held her still with a hand on the small of her back. He buried his other hand in her hair and arched her over his arm. Both of her breasts were thrust up at him. He had a lap full of woman and he knew that he wanted Justine more than he'd wanted any other woman in a long time.

Her eyes were closed, her hips moving subtly against him,

and when he blew on her nipple, he saw gooseflesh spread down her body.

He loved the way she reacted to his mouth on her breast. He kept his attention on her breasts. Her nipples were so sensitive, he was pretty sure he could bring her to orgasm just from touching her there.

The globes of her breasts were full and fleshy, more than a handful. He hardened as he wondered what his cock would feel like thrust between them.

He leaned down and licked the valley between her breasts, imagining his cock sliding back and forth there. He'd swell and she'd moan his name, watching him.

He bit carefully at the lily-white skin of her chest, suckling at her so that he'd leave his mark. He wanted her to remember this moment and what they had done when she was alone later.

He kept kissing and rubbing, pinching her nipples until her hands clenched in his hair and she rocked her hips harder against his length. He lifted his hips, thrusting up against her. He bit down carefully on her tender aroused nipple. She screamed his name and he hurriedly covered her mouth with his, wanting to feel every bit of her passion.

Rocking her until the storm passed and she quieted in his arms, he held her close, feeling her heartbeat against his chest and her soft exhalations against his neck. That she was letting him hold her was a pleasure he thought he'd never have.

He stroked his hands down her back and tried to keep from rushing her into another bout of sex. But he was desperate to get inside her silky body, and the feel of those bare breasts against his chest was driving him crazy.

He glanced down at her and saw she was watching him. The fire in her eyes made his entire body tight with anticipation. This was what he needed.

Justine was more to him than he'd thought he'd find. He

knew this evening was going to be rough. And he was honest enough to admit he was scared for the both of them. He didn't want to think of anything happening to Justine, and he really didn't like it that her job was one where she put herself in danger daily.

But that didn't matter right now. Now he was making love to her, Justine O'Neill . . . his woman, he thought. But he knew better than to say that out loud to her.

He refused to have sex with her again without using a condom. He put the condom on one-handed and reached for her again. He'd never wanted a woman the way he wanted Justine. There was something almost primal in the way he needed her.

"Hurry," she said, no shadows in her eyes now. "I don't know how long I can last," she said. "I really want you. Come to me now."

Her honest need for him was the sexiest thing he'd ever heard. It made him realize how much he needed her, and not just physically. He knew they both still had secrets, but right now, those secrets didn't matter.

Shifting on his lap, she settled her creamy pussy over his cock. She rubbed herself against his cock and he tightened his lower body, spasming as he shifted against her.

She reached between his legs and fondled his sac. As she cupped him in her hands, he shuddered. He needed to be inside her now. He shifted and lifted her thighs, wrapping her legs around his waist. Her hands fluttered between them and their eyes met.

He held her hips steady and entered her slowly, thrusting upward until he was fully seated. Her eyes widened with each inch he gave her. She clutched at his hips as he started thrusting. She held him to her, her eyes half-closed, head tipped back.

He couldn't resist the long length of her neck. He leaned down, biting carefully against her skin, and felt her shiver in his arms.

"Yes, Nigel, bite me again," she said.

And he did, enjoying the taste of her on his tongue and the feel of her in his arms.

He leaned up and caught one of her nipples in his teeth, scraping very gently. She started to tighten around him. Her hips moving faster, demanding more, but he kept the pace slow, steady, wanting her to come before he did.

He suckled her nipple and rotated his hips to catch her pleasure point with each thrust, and he felt her hands in his hair clenching as she threw her head back and her climax ripped through her.

He varied his thrusts, finding a rhythm that would draw out the tension at the base of his spine. Something that would make his time in her body, wrapped in her silky limbs, last forever.

He held her hips to him to give him deeper access to her body. Then she scraped her nails down his back, clutching his buttocks, drawing him in. His sac tightened and blood roared in his ears, as he felt everything in his world center on this one woman.

And he called her name as he came. He knew then that he was going to have a very difficult time giving her up, and he hoped that this relationship could survive once he was back to his normal life and he had his daughter with him again.

It bothered him that the woman he wanted so badly and needed the way he did pulled away the moment he dropped his arms. She got to her feet and dressed quickly. He didn't allow himself to get offended, simply got up and took a shower. When he came out of the bathroom, there were dark clothes laid out for him, and a note that said thank you.

He smiled to himself at the thought that she was once again thanking him for making love to her.

Chapter Thirteen

Justine looked again at the clock, waiting until it was time to go to the compound to meet Emile. She found herself in the kitchen and she knew what she wanted to try, but the last time she'd attempted to cook, it had been a full-blown disaster. There was no way she was trying again now.

Except they had three hours in front of them, and she'd already checked in with everyone about a dozen times. And if she wasn't careful, she was going to sit by Nigel on the couch again, but this time she wasn't going to have sex with him. No, this time she'd do something far more dangerous, like sit down next to him and put her head on his shoulder.

And then she'd never leave.

So it seemed like the lesser of two evils to open the cabinet and try to make a batch of cookies. Cookies were a normal girl thing. She and her sister had never made them, but they'd always talked about doing it. And Charity and Anna had at one time or another brought in cookies, usually around Christmas and birthdays.

So she stood there in front of the cupboard with the door open, staring at the containers marked flour and sugar.

"What are you doing?" Nigel asked, coming up behind her.

She jerked like he'd caught her doing something illegal. "Nothing."

"Hungry? I'm a fair cook. I can make you something."

"You can cook?" she asked. She couldn't even do that. Forget cookies, her dinners consisted of microwaveable specials.

She shook her head. "I'm not hungry."

She started to move away from him, but he put his arm around her waist and kept her close. She relaxed for just a second, leaning against him and resting her head on his shoulder.

"I can't cook," she said.

"So? You can kick butt and shoot a gun like nobody's business," he said.

"Well, that's not really helpful when it comes to doing the girlie things. The things that women are supposed to do."

"Like what?" Nigel asked.

She rolled her eyes at him. Was he really unsure, or did he simply want her to say it so he'd know she knew? "Cooking, cleaning, all those womanly things."

"I don't think those chores make you womanly."

"Every man does," Justine said.

What the hell was wrong with her? Was she really going to argue with him about this? She needed to just let it go. To just let him say his piece and then walk away. She would clean her gun again. That was something she could do, and it didn't require talking or cooking.

"Maybe because I'm British, I look at women differently."

She shrugged. "Maybe."

"Where did you get those ideas from?" Nigel asked.

"I don't know," she said at first, but then she remembered they had come from Franklin.

That he had said she wasn't going to be worth anything as a woman because she couldn't really cook, and wasn't very feminine.

It bothered her more than she wanted to admit that Franklin Baron was the reason she felt like a failure when it came to making cookies.

That she was trying to prove that anything that bastard said was wrong made her feel like a complete idiot.

"It was my stepfather."

"Stepfathers don't always get it right."

"He got a lot of other things wrong, too. I don't know why I was clinging to that idea like it was the truth."

"I don't know. Do you want to talk to me about whatever happened to you in the bedroom to make you not comfortable with making love?"

"I am comfortable with it. I haven't had any inappropriate reactions to you."

He rubbed his hand up and down on her arm. "No, you haven't, but you always jump out of my arms after we make love and get dressed as fast as you can.

"I'm not comfortable being nude," she said. She wanted to leave it at that. She couldn't even get changed at the gym in town when she went to work out. She just didn't like to get caught naked. It had nothing to do with her scars, and everything to do with the sexual way that Franklin had looked at her.

And he had ogled her each time she'd been partially dressed.

"I love your body, love. The next time we make love, I'm going to want to hold you in my arms afterward."

She thought about it. She could try to stay there for his sake. And she did want to hold him. She liked touching his body.

"Okay, I'll try it next time. I didn't think you'd want to linger after," she said. "Most men don't."

"Well, I do. I like a nice cuddle after making love."

"Are you ready to go get Piper?" she asked.

"As ready as I'll ever be. Is Charity close by?"

"Yes. She's going to meet us at the compound and provide cover when we go in. Anna's on her way and will provide backup."

They had been drinking water and taking it easy all afternoon, letting their bodies acclimate to the higher altitude.

And now she realized she might have to acclimate to something else. She might need to acclimate to Nigel. And she didn't know if that was safe. She didn't know if being comfortable with this one man was going to be the right thing for her.

Nigel made dinner for Justine and himself, thinking that would ease her worries about cooking, but instead, it seemed to make her quieter. He wasn't nervous about going after Piper. Action was what they both needed and he suspected she knew it, too. He would have liked to have made love to her one more time.

Anything to cement the bond between them, but another part of him thought it might be better to just let things lie. To just let Justine and he remain essentially strangers who'd shared a couple of really intense moments.

"Thanks for making this," she said.

"It was nothing. I learned to cook a long time ago—couldn't face another boxed dinner."

"That's what I have most every night," she said.

And he knew he'd said the wrong thing again. But Justine wasn't like other women he'd dated in the past, and she never reacted the way he expected her to.

"Well, there is nothing wrong with that."

"I know," she said. She wandered around the small kitchen area, stopping to open drawers and fiddle with their contents. "Have you thought any more about the initials on the note?"

"Yes, actually I did. Can Anna send us an image of the fax? Maybe seeing the way it's written will jar something for me."

"Yes, she can."

Justine put her fork down and called her friend. But there was no satellite signal and she had to leave a message. Anna's computer genius had saved the day more than once, and Justine knew if there was a way for her to make something happen in this case, she'd do it.

Anna had been kidnapped as a young girl, and that event had made her determined to try to keep other kids from being kidnapped. Anna was a child of privilege, and she'd always said there was more responsibility than money in her background.

Having been on the rough terrain, he now understood why they'd lost the signal to Constance and Piper a few times. As convenient as cell phones were, he knew they made life damned inconvenient when they didn't work. And right now, he thought he should come up with a device that would enable them to work wherever you were in the world. Even a jungle in the Amazon Basin.

"Once we have Piper, where are we going?"

"There is a second safe house that I think we should take her to, just in case this location has been compromised. I'll show you where it is on the way out."

"You don't have to," Nigel said. He wanted to concentrate on what was happening later tonight, and he really didn't want to imagine being separated from Justine. He needed her by his side.

"It's just in case anything happens to me. In fact, you should have Charity and Anna's cell phone numbers," she said, rattling them both off. He saw she had that look in her eye that meant she was focused on work again. And her career meant a lot to her.

To him it meant she wasn't thinking about her failures as a woman again. And he had the feeling she viewed things like not being able to cook as a failure.

He wished he knew who her stepfather was. Anyone who was in the paternal role needed to put aside his own petty ideas about what an ideal child was, and realize that kids were unique and different. And they needed to be shown that whatever they were good at doing was enough. That each person in society was good at something different, so they could all make up a whole.

"You are staring at me again. You do that a lot."

"Well, you are very pretty."

"I'm not. I'm not even classically beautiful. Everyone always says how gorgeous Charity is."

"What do they say about you?"

"How good I am with the weapons," she said.

"You are good with that, but you are also very beautiful. Even Piper thought so."

"Well, I don't think a eight- or nine-year-old girl is really the best judge."

"Oh, but kids are. They don't lie unless they've been taught to."

Justine watched him with her gray fairy eyes, and he felt like she was stripping him bare, all the way to his soul.

"How do you teach someone to lie?" she asked. She really had no idea how that habit was formed.

"By always lying to them," Nigel said. "Are you done with dinner?"

She stood up and took his plate. It was the least she could do after he went to the trouble of making dinner. She knew Nigel wasn't judging her and she appreciated that, but she was judging herself and she knew she came up lacking. She'd been coming up lacking in the woman department for a long time.

A few minutes later, her BlackBerry beeped and she realized she had a message waiting. She opened the attachment in her email, and saw it was from Anna. She went into the dining room where Nigel stood looking out into the jungle-filled backyard. They weren't quite in the Amazon Basin here, but they were close enough for the vegetation to start creeping into the cleared-out space.

"Here's the fax. Does this signature or handwriting jar anything for you?"

He glanced at it. She watched him studying the signature and waited. "It looks familiar to me. Let me see the list of former Baron employees."

She pulled up the scanned image so he could see it, and looked over his shoulder while he looked at it. None of the names were the same. But Nigel saw something.

"Have Anna run a background on Marshall Fermann."

"Who is he?" Justine asked while sending the note to Anna.

"He was my assistant nearly a year ago. He left in the middle of a merger with Johnson Ellis Brands. They were a small pharmaceutical house."

"Why did he leave?"

"He thought he would be promoted and given the new company to run."

"How certain are you that he's our guy?" Justine asked. She needed to know where they stood.

"He's the one. He made a few threats on his last day, and left a note blaming me for ruining his life."

"Why didn't you think of him before?"

"The man wasn't self-motivated. That was the main reason I didn't want him in charge of any operation we had. He just didn't have the balls to really go to the wall for our company."

"Seems like he wants to prove to you that he's changed."

"Seems that way," Nigel said. "But once a person reaches adulthood, they really don't change. I think with Marshall, it's a case of being so focused on hating me that that's all he can do. He'll never be able to adapt to the marketplace again."

Justine agreed with Nigel's assessment. But it gave her a

chill to do so. She could tell from the way he was talking that he believed no one could change has an adult, and her entire adult existence had been about proving she was more than the juvenile killer she had been.

They left the car half a mile from the compound and went on foot through the jungle terrain, up to the complex where Piper and Constance were being held.

"Remember when we get there that this might be a trap. You have to listen to me and Charity. She'll tell you when it's clear to move. If she says to drop to the ground or to run, you do what she says."

"I will," he said, his accent crisp.

"I'm not saying this to yank your chain, but if you die, then who will Piper have?"

"I know that, Justine."

She didn't say anything else until Charity came on. "I'm in position. You have a guard unit in front of your position, and they are walking away. From what I observed earlier, they move in intervals that bring them by that exact spot every ten minutes.

"We've just wasted a few minutes," Justine said. "We'll move after the next unit goes past."

Justine took Nigel's arm, pulling him further into the brush behind the house. They were both equipped with rappelling hooks and rope they would use to climb over the wall.

They watched the armed men with the guns on their back circle the grounds. The men were clearly guards, and obviously knew what they were doing.

Justine realized they'd found the mercenaries Marshall had hired. She hoped that Emile had a way of distracting the man or men who were guarding Piper. Because otherwise, she was going to have a real struggle getting the better of these guys.

It would be just the kind of fight she didn't want, with a little girl caught in the middle of another firefight, like they'd had yesterday at the airport. Had it really only been a day since they'd gotten to Peru? It felt like a lifetime had passed.

Night fell early in the mountains, and Justine was ready to move as soon as it was fully dark. She had on her special earpiece that was modulated so she could communicate with Charity and Anna. Nigel had one on, too. They'd tested them at the house before they left.

"Ready?" she asked, keeping her voice low and monotone.

"Yes," he replied. She took the rappelling hook and rope she'd brought and tossed it up to the top of the fence. They both climbed up and over the fence, dropping down on the other side. Having Nigel by her side was the first time she didn't mind having a partner. And he was starting to seem more a partner in this endeavor than a client.

He had changed to fit the circumstances, something she suspected he did a lot of. She could see now why he was such a good executive, and imagined that was part of the reason he was such a good father.

Piper was well-adjusted to her lifestyle because of Nigel, and that was the first time Justine had ever seen a parent change and adapt to fit the needs of their child.

"What now?" Nigel asked.

"We wait for a signal from Emile. We don't want to move on the house unless we can be certain that Piper won't be harmed." She took out her night-vision goggles and put them on. She glanced at Nigel, and saw him fumbling with his.

"What's the matter?"

"Nothing."

"Are you nervous?"

"No. But being so close to Piper . . . all I want is to storm in there and get her. I need to hold her and make sure she's safe."

"Soon," Justine said. She drew Nigel back into the shadows as a unit of two guards started making the rounds. "Charity?"

"I'm here," she said. She was monitoring the comings and goings at the compound from a little ways up the mountain.

"Do you see anything?"

"No. The guard unit is almost on your position. Once they pass, you can move toward the house. Go in silently."

She motioned to Nigel to keep quiet while they waited for the guard unit to pass. Once the men were out of their line of sight, they both stood up and moved quickly toward the house closest to them. They kept low, and Justine was once again impressed with Nigel's skills.

The man knew how to stay alive, and she realized he was a survivor like she was. She thought about what he'd said in the car on the drive over to Cusco, about being left behind by his mother. That incident had clearly shaped him into the man he was today.

"Hold your position," Charity said. "You've got company moving toward you."

"Pair?" Justine asked, pulling her knife from her chest sheath.

"Single."

"Stay put, Nigel. I'm going to drop back so I can surprise whoever it is."

He nodded and stayed where he was while she moved back into the shadows. She realized how at home she was in the shadows. This was the world where she knew what to do. It didn't matter that she couldn't cook now, because she did know how to save lives, how to protect the innocent and make sure the wicked went straight to hell.

Okay, enough with the melodrama, she thought.

She heard the footsteps and saw the heavy shadow move past her. She attacked, taking the man down and putting her knife against his jugular.

"It's me, Emile."

"Emile, why didn't you signal?"

"I'm being watched. They've moved the girl. Get off me. We have no time to lose."

She got up, and Emile got to his feet next to her. Nigel had his gun leveled at both of them.

Justine nodded at him, proud of the way he had known what to do without her telling him.

"We have no time to lose. The girl is being held in the basement of the second house over there. Follow me," Emile said.

They stayed to the shadows, following Emile. Justine drew her gun, keeping it at the ready. She wasn't too sure that Emile wasn't leading them into a trap. It was nice to know that being with Nigel wasn't making her lose her edge. She still didn't trust anyone.

But she realized she was just starting to trust Nigel, and that thought was a little scary, but comforting.

Chapter Fourteen

"In there, and then down to the basement," Emile said. Nigel was halfway through the door before he remembered what Justine had warned him about. This could be a trap. He pulled up and scanned the room before entering, letting his gun lead the way. He stepped through the doorway once he ascertained the room was clear, and then he walked across the floor. There were no sounds in the house, and it was dark. He would have thought the place was abandoned.

"Can you get a thermal image of the house?" Justine asked.

"I'm working on it. The computer is giving me fits . . ." Charity said. "I think it's because of the humidity."

"Emile is back outside," Charity said. "Keep me posted on your whereabouts."

"I will."

She motioned to Nigel that she'd go first. She opened the door Emile had indicated, and saw that it did indeed lead to a basement. She had no idea how many stairs there were, and she wasn't going to turn on the light. Couldn't chance alerting whoever was at the bottom that they were coming. She didn't like the way this entire setup felt.

But turning back wasn't an option.

"Wait here," she said to Nigel.

"Why?"

"I need to make sure this isn't a trap. Keep your gun drawn and watch my back."

"I . . . will do," he said.

She knew he wanted to be the one to go down into the basement and find Piper, but she had no idea what they'd be facing. Justine made her way carefully down the stairs, keeping her gun drawn with the safety off. She went down until she felt the concrete floor beneath her feet, and then started making a perimeter around the room. She went less than five feet before she encountered something on the floor. A body.

She dropped to one knee and felt around the body. Searching for the head and a pulse. Instead, she found congealed blood on a cold lifeless body.

"I've got a dead body in here—not Piper."

"I'm coming down," Nigel said.

"No. Stay there. I don't think Piper is here. Charity, did you see where Emile went?"

"Yes. Back to the main building."

Piper pulled out a small penlight and flicked it on, keeping her weapon at the ready to fire. She scanned the room and found it empty except for the body, which she now saw was Constance.

"Constance is dead. Piper's not down here." She scanned the room further just in case she'd missed something.

She felt impotent at finding Constance too late. Where the hell was Piper, and why had Emile led them here? "Is there anything unusual outside, Charity?"

"Not that I can tell. There are about eight men in the building next to where you are."

"I'm coming up behind you, Nigel."

"We can't leave Constance here," he said.

"We will come back for her," Justine said. "Our focus is on Piper."

"You're right," Nigel said. "Where to next?"

"Charity?"

"I'd head to the right. There are two images in the building next to you. It's hard to tell if they are adult or child because they are seated," Charity said.

"Check on Piper's GPS, Charity," Justine said.

"The signal is still here. I'm monitoring it, and will let you know if there is movement."

"To the right then?" Nigel asked.

"Yes. To the right. We'll go low again like we did before, and stay alert."

"I will."

Justine led the way, with Nigel right on her back. She kicked opened the door to the next building and scanned the room with her gun, then entered. There was one man in the corner who dropped a book and then reached for his gun. He pulled it and fired, hitting the frame of the doorway, and a sliver of wood caught her on her left cheek. She felt the sting as she lifted her gun and returned fire. She heard Nigel step inside and close the door behind him.

Justine hit the man and he fell to the floor. She moved quickly to bind his hands and feet with flex cuffs. She trusted Nigel at her back.

"There's one more person in the building, moving toward your position."

"I've got them," Nigel said.

Justine finished securing the guard she'd taken out. "Where is the girl being held?"

The man stared up at her blankly, so she repeated her question in Spanish.

"I will tell you nothing."

Justine drew back her hand and hit the man with the butt of the gun. "Are you sure?"

Blood dripped from his nose and his upper lip was swollen. "Yes."

She hit him again, this time to knock him out. She got to her feet as another guard entered the room. Nigel stepped up behind the man and put his gun to the back of the man's head. "Drop your weapons."

The man did as ordered. "Get on your knees, hands behind your head."

Once the man was secure, Justine asked him where the girl was and again got no response. Nigel surprised her by grabbing the man by the back of his head and putting the barrel of his weapon on the man's chin.

"Tell me where the girl is being kept or you will die."

Nigel was tired and frustrated, and at this point he didn't care what he had to do. If they didn't find Piper soon, he was going to give in to the berserk rage that was boiling up inside of him, and lay waste to this entire complex.

He was more than angry that that stupid git Marshall had concocted a plan like this, threatening Piper, all because the man hadn't been promoted. He should have made the connection sooner, Nigel thought.

But he hadn't, and there was nothing more he could about it now.

"I don't know where the child is. She was next door, but this evening she was moved."

"Why?"

"Do I look like someone who the boss discusses his plans with?"

Nigel drew back his hand and hit the man hard. His knuckles ached a little afterward, but it felt good. They stuffed a rag Justine had found in the kitchen in the captive's mouth.

"You've got three units moving toward your position. You are clear to go out the back door if you move fast."

"We're out," Justine said. Nigel was on her heels as they stepped outside. The night air was heavy with humidity and the smell of jungle vegetation.

"I'm pissed as hell," Nigel said.

"We all are. It sounds like Emile was being watched," Justine said.

"How much firepower do you have on you, Justine?" Charity asked.

"Just two semiautomatics and three replacement clips. Why?"

"There are too many people in the other building for just the two of you to clear it. I think your best bet is to clear out."

"I'm not leaving without Piper," Nigel said.

"Wait a minute. Something's going on. They are mobilizing," Charity said.

Justine turned and saw two men covering a third man, who was carrying a bundle wrapped in a blanket—a bundle that looked a lot like Piper. As the men ran toward the Jeep, Justine drew her gun and took out the first guard. The second one returned fire and she took a hit in her upper thigh. It burned like hell, but she kept moving. She wasn't as fast as she'd been earlier. Nigel was right on her trail and opened fire. His shots weren't as accurate as they had been earlier, and she put that down to worry about hitting his daughter. Justine hit the man carrying the bundle right between the eyes and watched him collapse. He dropped the bundle.

Nigel ran forward, heedless of what was going on around them. But when he got there, he found the blankets were empty, save for Piper's stuffed bunny. No wonder the GPS was staying still—the bunny was here, but Piper was gone.

"Fuck."

"No kid?" Charity asked.

"Just the bunny with the GPS."

"Okay, let's think," Charity said.

"I'm going to find the security headquarters. We can't just kill the remaining guards. Someone has to know something," Justine said.

Nigel picked up the small stuffed animal and cradled it in his arms for a second before tucking it under his shirt, where he could keep his hands free.

"What's next?"

"We need to find someone who will talk. And I want Emile," Justine said.

Anna's voice came on their comm-link. "Emile is with the girl. Sorry for the double-cross. It was a test."

"Is she okay?"

"She's alive, as near as Emile could tell. That was all he could give me."

"Why did he—"

"Not now, Nigel. We'll have time to get our questions answered later."

Justine knew they had to keep moving. She directed Nigel out of the compound and away from the six men who were still searching for them. She heard the sound of a Jeep starting.

"Move it, Nigel. We need to be in the car as soon as possible."

He ran beside her and in a few moments they were both safely back in the Humvee. Her leg hurt like a mother.

"Anna, are you still there?" Justine asked as she reached into the backseat to grab her medical kit.

"Yes."

"Did Emile indicate where they are going?" Justine asked. "Nigel, can you help me with this?"

"Out of the city and into the jungle," Anna said.

"Yes," Nigel said. "Give me the medical pack and I'll take care of it."

"What's wrong? Who's hurt?" Charity asked.

"Justine. Her leg is bleeding."

"It's a bullet wound, but it went straight through. I just need to patch the entrance and exit wounds and then I'll wrap it," Justine said.

"Does he have a GPS signal we can track?" Justine asked Anna.

"Yes. I'm patching it through to your BlackBerry. Wait for Charity. You'll need the extra manpower."

"Where is he headed?" Nigel asked as he worked on her leg. He was gentler than she would have been. He cut away the fabric around the wound and cleaned the area before he bandaged it. He wrapped the leg tightly in an Ace bandage.

"It looks like the new Baron plant. I'm on route to intercept," Anna said.

"I'll call the security team that's there and alert them," Charity said.

"We might have a better chance of catching them in the jungle if you can get them to abandon their car," Justine said. "Thanks, Nigel. I'm good as new now."

The wound was just a surface one and not too deep. Nigel dabbed at her face with the antiseptic. "The jungle isn't very kind to open wounds."

He bandaged her forehead and then kissed her. "I think you're all patched up now."

"Thanks, Nigel," Anna said.

"No problem. About them ditching the vehicle . . . I don't think it'll be that hard. They've had flooding rains in recent weeks," Nigel said. "That's part of why we were behind schedule."

"Were your workers even striking?"

"Yes. Some local was protesting and the workers stayed away."

"Do you think it was Marshall?" Justine asked him.

Nigel shrugged.

"How does he have the money to do all this?" Charity asked.

"He got a very nice severance package when he left Baron," Nigel said.

"And his grandfather owns most of the land around here," Anna added. "I think he has influence over the people here because he can threaten their lifestyle."

They were moving again, following a blinking signal on the GPS map. Justine suspected that Nigel had to be frustrated by how close they'd come to finding his daughter.

Nigel didn't say much as the women talked about plans. He just held Piper's bunny in one hand and his gun in the other. This was what his life had come down to. And he realized that even though he'd believed he'd left the past behind, his life hadn't really changed.

His cell phone rang and he removed his earpiece to answer it. "This is Nigel Carter."

"It's Derrick. Did you get the list I sent to you this morning?"

"Yes, thank you. It was very helpful. Do have any contact information for Marshall Fermann?"

"Yes. He's on linkedin.com with me as one of my connections."

Nigel was familiar with the social website. A lot of companies, including his own, used the site to recruit and search for talent.

"Should I tell him you are trying to get in touch with him?" Derrick asked.

"Yes. I'd like to talk to him if I can."

"How are things going in Peru? Is the compound as bad off as we suspected?"

It was the first time Derrick had asked a question about the

company and their business without sounding scared or unsure. So maybe that was why Nigel decided not to tell him
anything that was going on. "Everything is fine here. The security team is top rate."

"Oh, that's good to hear."

Derrick hung up a few minutes later.

"How certain are we that Marshall is the man behind this?"

"Why?"

"Because Derrick didn't sound like himself just now."

"What was different?"

"The questions he asked."

"How is that different?"

"The man never asks questions and always sounds like he's
afraid of his own shadow, but today he didn't."

"Anna, run a check on Derrick Baron. See if he has any contacts here, okay?"

Nigel put his earpiece back in and heard Anna say that she
was on it.

He was glad to know the team was working to get Piper
back, but he needed her here now. He needed results, and to
be honest, he knew that the women were doing all they could
to get the work done.

Justine didn't go back to the safe house, just kept the
Humvee moving, following that flashing GPS beacon. He
knew she was as frustrated as he was.

"What about Constance?"

"Sam is taking care of her. Her body will be retrieved and
returned to the States."

Nigel was sad to think of Piper's nanny dead. He and Constance had been on the same wavelength as far as the care of
Piper had been concerned, and she had been a funny woman.
A little dry in her sense of humor, but he'd liked her. And he
would miss her.

"How far is it to your factory?"

"Not too much farther. But the road is supposedly impassable once we leave the city," Nigel said.

"Charity?"

"Yes."

"Can you get a satellite image of the road up ahead? Are we going to be able to drive to the factory?"

"Just a second," Charity said.

"I'm sorry, Nigel. I wish we had—"

"Don't apologize. The fact that he's one step ahead of us isn't something we can control. We will get him and Piper—that's all that matters."

But deep inside he was almost afraid to believe that they would get her back. Her bunny was mangled and Constance was dead, and his little girl was all alone.

The one thing he'd never wanted for her.

He'd worked hard to ensure she'd always be safe and never have to take care of herself the way he'd had to. But now he prayed Piper had the same instincts he'd had. That she was able to keep it together and stay alive until he got to her.

"The road is out up ahead, and I think they had to abandon their vehicle as well. The signal is still moving, but the pace is slower," Charity said.

"How do you feel about a jungle trek?" Justine asked.

"I'll do whatever it takes."

"I thought you'd say that. Will you look in that black bag in the backseat for a machete?"

"Why do we need a machete?"

"It's the only thing that really works in the jungle. Paths don't really last long."

"Have you been down here before?"

"A few times Sam has taken a job where we go in and rescue missionaries, or kidnapped college kids. Stuff like that. I know a good bit about the jungle," Justine said.

"I know the cement jungles of the world, and can handle my own in them, but this kind of place—Wait—

"What?"

"Don't follow the trail they are leading us on. We can go another twenty miles south and take the new access road."

"Are you sure it's open?" Justine asked.

"Positive. I paid extra to have that area filled in and paved. Charity, will you check the coordinates on the satellite?"

Nigel gave her the longitude and latitude of the new road they'd just had built.

"It looks open. In fact, my security team says they've been using it this morning."

"Good," Nigel said.

"I've got an idea," Justine said. "A way we can stop being the followers and get a jump on Piper and her kidnappers."

"You don't think it's Marshall anymore?" Nigel asked.

"I don't know, and I don't want to make any more mistakes. And I know that the Baron men are capable of unspeakable things."

Nigel knew there was a lot more to this conversation than what Justine was letting on. There was real malice in her voice when she talked about Baron Industries, and he remembered when they'd first met at the Baron offices.

What was the connection to Baron and Justine? Or was it simply that she didn't like big business. He wasn't going to let this rest until he found out everything he could.

Chapter Fifteen

"What kind of unspeakable acts?"

Justine shook her head. "Just dirty business dealings."

Nigel got very quiet and still. "How do you know that?"

"It was in the file," Charity said. "Sam's information is top rate."

Justine hadn't realized that Sam had included past practices in the file he'd given them. She should have, though. He was thorough. The only reason she hadn't read the file was because she couldn't tolerate anything that had to do with Baron Industries.

She glanced at Nigel and realized that wasn't true anymore. She did care a great deal about Nigel, and it didn't matter to her that he was a part of Baron. She knew that Nigel wasn't doing anything illegal, and that he wouldn't. She had learned the measure of the man Nigel was, and he was someone she could respect.

"What?" he asked, looking up at her as she stared at him.

"I just realized that you are the kind of man I didn't think existed anymore," Justine said.

"What kind of man is that?" Charity asked.

"I'm going silent for a few minutes."

"Don't. There isn't time for you to have a personal conversation with Nigel," Anna said.

Nigel was looking at her now like she'd surprised him.

"You guys are right. What's the plan?"

He put his hand on her thigh right near where the bandage was. Muting the microphone on his earpiece he looked at her. "You surprised me, too."

"I . . ."

"Justine, we are almost to your location. We will meet up and discuss in person."

"Sounds good," Justine said. She took her earpiece out and shut it off, realizing this might be the last time she was alone with Nigel. She looked at him and there was still so much she had to say. Parts of her past that she should probably tell him about, but the past didn't seem important just now.

She remembered the way he'd been earlier when they'd been searching the compound for Piper. She admired the way he'd kept cool under pressure. She leaned across the seat and drew him to her. This time, there was no reason why they couldn't embrace.

She didn't feel trapped in the car the way she had beside that hut. Here, she just kissed him and held him close to her, trying to convey without words all that she was feeling.

She liked the feel of his hand against her face. He made her feel cherished and beautiful, two things she could safely say she'd never experienced before.

Even now, when she'd just come back from doing things that most men would find repulsive, he held her close to him. He made her feel womanly just being in his arms.

She knew they didn't have time for this, but she needed something from him. Needed to feel his body pressed against hers, even here in the front seat of the Humvee, while Anna and Charity were on their way.

Nigel drew her more fully against him, kissing her slowly, thoroughly, and very deeply. He caught her earlobe between his teeth and breathed into her ear as he said, "I want you now."

"Here?" she asked, but it was what she wanted and needed, too. There was something about Nigel that made her forget that she wasn't a physical person, that she didn't need sex or intimacy, because with him she needed it all.

Nigel didn't waste time on slow seduction. "Get your pants off."

She reached for her zipper and noticed he did the same. He lowered his pants enough to free his cock. She pushed hers down her thighs and to her ankles, the fabric trapped by her boots. He lifted her onto his lap so that she sat facing away from him.

The movement thrust her breasts forward. The T-shirt and Kevlar vest still completely covered her torso, but a moment later she felt his hand on her shirt, drawing it up and off her body, and then the vest and bra followed. Soon he was cupping her bare breasts in his hands. She parted her legs and he groaned her name. Blood rushed through his veins, pooling in his groin.

"Yes, love."

She shifted on him and he felt her moisture on the tip of his cock. Her legs shifted restlessly around his hips. Though it had been just last night when he'd had her, it felt like an eternity since he'd last held her in his arms.

He'd been aroused since they'd both escaped the compound with their lives. He had come so close to losing everything and to having everything tonight, and he needed to make love to Justine to remind himself that he was still alive.

She twisted her head so that their lips could meet. Her mouth opened under his and he told himself to take it slow, but slow wasn't in his programming with this woman. And they didn't have time for extended lovemaking. He should just thrust into her and come, but he wanted—no, needed—to ensure her pleasure first.

Justine was pure feminine temptation and he had her in his arms. He slid his hands down her back, caressing the long smooth line of her back. There were two small scars on her back. Little pucker wounds that looked like they had been caused by a gunshot.

He rubbed his finger over them a few times, then let his hands drop lower, caressing the full cheeks of her buttocks.

He rubbed the crown of his cock against her feminine mound from behind. He felt the humid warmth at her center on his flesh and moaned out loud. He reached between them to caress that slit between her legs. She was creamy and hot with desire. He caressed the edge of her body. She shifted more fully into him.

Her breasts rose and fell as she breathed heavily. He saw the barest hint of the rosy flesh of her nipples as he looked over her shoulder. He wanted to take those nipples in his mouth, but contented himself with caressing them with his fingers.

Her nipples stood out. He ran the tip of one fingertip around her aroused flesh. She trembled in his arms.

Lowering his head, he bit gently at the back of her neck, suckling the skin there. She brought one hand up to cup the back of his neck and held him to her with a strength that surprised him, but shouldn't have.

Her fingers drifted down his arm and blood roared in his ear. He was so hard, so full right now, that he needed to be inside her body.

God, she was soft. She moaned as he neared her center and then sighed when he brushed his fingertips across the entrance to her body.

The area was warm and wet. He slipped one finger into her

and hesitated for a second as she glanced back over her shoulder at him.

Her eyes were heavy-lidded. She bit down on her lower lip, and he felt the minute movements of her hips as she tried to move his touch where she needed it.

He was beyond teasing her or prolonging anything. He plunged two fingers into her humid body. She squirmed against him.

He needed her *now*. He shifted her on his body and thrust upward with his hips. She pushed back against him, but he wasn't ready to enter her yet. Their naked loins pressed together and he shook under the impact.

He had to have her. *Now*. He cupped both of her breasts in his hands, plucking at her aroused nipples. He slipped one hand down her body, testing the readiness of her desire for him. He found her wet and ready. He adjusted his stance, bending his knees and positioning himself, and then entered her with one long, hard stroke.

She moaned his name and her head fell forward, leaving the curve of her neck open and vulnerable to him. He bit at her neck softly, and felt her reaction all the way to his toes when she squirmed in his arms and thrust her hips back toward him.

A tingling started in the base of his spine, and he knew his climax was close. But he wasn't going without Justine. He wanted her with him. He caressed her stomach and her breasts, whispered erotic words of praise and longing in her ears.

She moved more frantically in his arms and he shafted her deep with each stroke. Breathing out through his mouth, he tried to hold back the inevitable. He slid one hand down her abdomen, through the slick folds of her sex, finding her center. He stroked the aroused flesh with an up-and-down movement. She continued to writhe in his arms, but was no closer to climax than before.

He circled that aroused bit of flesh between her legs with his forefinger, than scraped it very carefully with his nail. She screamed his name and tightened around his cock. Nigel pulled one hand from her body, locked his fingers on the cool railing next to her small hand, then penetrated her as deeply as he could. Biting down on the back of her neck, he came long and hard.

He caught her chin in his hands and turned her toward him. Bringing her so that their eyes met, he knew he wasn't going to be able to walk away from her when this was over. No matter what happened with Piper, he couldn't envision his future without Justine by his side. But he hadn't gotten to be the CEO of Baron Industries by being a stupid man, and he knew Justine was never going to be content to be his wife. That was what all the worrying about cooking was about. But at this moment when he held her in his arms, he didn't worry about anything but holding her.

Justine hurried back into her clothes, realizing once again that Nigel had come inside her. She probably should have said something to him the first time he had. She was on the pill, so pregnancy wasn't a problem, and she was disease-free.

A part of her liked having his semen inside her. It was a part of Nigel that she'd carry around with her.

Her cell phone rang and she answered it.

"Why did you take off your earpiece?"

"Because I wanted to have a conversation without you and Anna listening in. Where are you guys?"

"Almost to the factory. We will meet you there."

"Okay. We stopped for a moment, but will be right behind you."

"Is everything okay with you?" Charity asked.

Justine had no idea. She hadn't ever really been okay; she'd just found a way to live in a kind of numbness, but now all that had changed. Nigel had knocked her out of that numbness, and a part of her was scared that she'd never find her way back to it.

"I'm fine. We'll be there in a few minutes."

"Anna is on the phone with Emile."

"What's up?"

"I don't know. Let me call you back."

Justine got back into the driver's seat.

"Was that your mates?"

"Yes. We need to get moving."

He nodded. She reached for the keys to start the car, but he stopped her with his hand on her wrist. "Are you okay?"

"Yes."

"No bad moments?"

"None at all. Thanks, Nigel. I can't . . . it means a lot to me."

"What does?"

"That you care," she said before she could censor her thoughts. But it was very true; it did mean a lot to her, the way he cared about her.

"I'm glad, and you're very welcome," he said. "Did Charity or Anna find out anything about Derrick?"

"No. They had nothing new to report. Just wondered why we were both silent."

"I notice you didn't tell them you were making love with me."

"Um . . . no. I'm not really the pour-your-heart-out kind of girl."

He tipped his head to the side, studying her for a moment. "No, you are definitely more of the cards-close-to-your-chest girl."

"What about you? How are you emotionally?" she asked.

They were both dressed again, and she put the car back in gear and finished driving up the road to the factory.

"I'm a guy . . . I don't do heart-on-my-sleeve. Except maybe where Piper is concerned. She's always known she owned me."

"Really?"

"Yes. Wasn't it that way with your father?"

Justine thought about that tough old marine who'd been her daddy, and she knew it had been true. "I guess you're right. I thought my dad hung the moon, and when he died, I was inconsolable."

"You mentioned a stepdad. Did he fill your father's shoes?"

"No. He wasn't anything like my father. I didn't get along with him at all."

"Why not?"

She took a deep breath and realized she was going to tell him about Franklin. She couldn't believe it, but she wanted him to know. Then, if he was disgusted by her past and what she'd done, she'd know it before things went too far.

"He wasn't a very nice man. He had a thing for little girls."

Nigel cursed under his breath and reached for her, then hesitated. "I'm sorry."

She shrugged. "There's more to it, but it just gets uglier."

"Tell me," he said.

"My mother wouldn't listen to me when I tried to tell her what was going on. So I just stopped talking about it. Then he turned his attention to my younger sister Millie, and I knew I couldn't . . . I just couldn't let him do to her what he'd done to me."

"What did you do?"

"I got my father's old military-issue knife, and waited for him to come to my room. When he did, I stabbed him in the heart. I was always this small, but my daddy used to make Millie and I defend ourselves, so I knew how to fight and fight dirty."

Justine stopped talking and the silence in the car felt awkward to her. But hearing the words out loud made a difference. She hadn't told anyone about that night since the judge had asked her what happened in juvenile court.

"Did you kill him?"

"Yes. My mom was horrified, and my sister was scared for me. I was arrested and tried as a juvenile. I was placed in a juvenile detention center and Millie was placed in foster care the next year."

"When did you get out of jail?"

"It was a juvenile sentence, so it meant I didn't have to serve time in a correctional facility. I was released from the detention center on my eighteenth birthday."

"How'd you get from there to here?" he asked.

How had she? She didn't really remember much of those first months out of the facility, but she'd had a hard time fitting in with other kids. She had become even more of a loner than she had been before she'd gone into the juvenile center.

Her life really changed when she'd started working in Jack's bar.

"I worked in bars as a bouncer. No one ever expected me to be able to do the job given my size, but I did. And one day I got a call from Sam. He knew about my record, but he'd also heard about some of the other things I'd done, like helping street kids and stuff like that, and he offered me training and then a job."

Nigel didn't say anything else and she was glad. She didn't know why she'd suddenly started talking. Oh, that was a big fat lie. She knew why.

She was starting to fall for Nigel Carter, and if him knowing she had killed a man like Franklin Baron was going to make a difference to him, she wanted to know now.

"I am humbled by you, Justine."

She shook her head. "Don't be. Killing like I did, it was necessary, but I don't think it was anything special. It made me into who I am today, and I can't—hell, I *won't* regret that. But you've seen me at my lowest. You know I don't know how to react properly all the time."

"That doesn't mean what you did was wrong, or even that your reactions are wrong," Nigel said, and he reached over to touch her face.

"Your reactions are your own, just like your past is. You can't be anything other than who you are."

Justine looked over at him and realized he had a point. She'd never apologized for her past, but she didn't wear it like a banner or a chip on her shoulder either. It was just a big chunk of who she was. She couldn't change it.

And it had enabled her to protect other people, which was something she really enjoyed. Her skills had developed in the facility where she'd studied different types of fighting. At first, she'd thought she'd be some kind of vigilante for kids like herself, who had no one else to turn to. She'd been doing that when Sam found her.

Sam had shown her there was justice to be found inside the law. Sometimes Justine didn't like the way the system worked because it was too slow. But she understood his point about being an agent for justice versus being a flat-out killer.

"I guess both of us were defined by our childhood," Justine said, then realized how that must make Nigel feel.

His daughter was going to be defined by this incident, whether he wanted her to be or not. There was no way that Piper was going to walk away from Peru unscathed by all that had happened to her.

All that Nigel could do would be to ensure that she had the grounding to keep herself in check.

"I think we all are," Nigel said. "Even the ones in the 'normal' households."

"What is normal?"

"I have no idea. Where I grew up, it was fatherless families and mums that worked two jobs. None of my mates in Essex had a parent home after school, did you?"

"No. I mean, my mom married into money so she didn't have to work, but she had a lot of social obligations and was rarely home for Millie and I in the afternoons."

"So neither of us is normal?" Nigel asked.

"I get what you're saying about normal being defined as what we are familiar with. But didn't you even think about having a mom and a dad? Didn't you ever want that Norman Rockwell picture of family?"

He shrugged. "I can't recall. Maybe at one time, but I got married and had a child. I have a good job and make a good wage, so if anyone should have had 'normal,' it's me. But I am a single dad whose daughter has been kidnapped . . .

He turned and looked at Justine. "I don't think there is anything regular about family life. I believe all families are normal in their own ways, and there is little we can do to change it."

Nigel knew he was going to implement more safety features into his family once he had Piper back. He would never be able to sleep again at night until he knew she was as safe as he could make her.

Chapter Sixteen

Alfred, the head of the security team at Baron's Cusco plant, had another envelope with Nigel's name on it. He collected it from the man before leading the Liberty Investigations team to the house his plant manager had been using. Charity didn't come with them, but instead wanted to stay focused on her mission, which was training the security staff. She would meet up with the rest of them later.

"Emile is concerned with his boss. He says the man wants to leave the girl in the jungle. I told Emile to leave his phone with her and we will trace it. I actually think Piper would do better on her own then with Marshall," Anna said.

"Why do you say that?" Nigel asked. But he, too, thought the sooner she was away from the captors, the better it would be for her.

"We can get to her quickly. And even drugged kids can remember things."

There was a note in Anna's voice that made it seem as if she knew from personal experience. "What did he say?"

"That he'd let us know what happened."

"I'm not sure we can trust him," Justine said.

"He isn't getting any money until he delivers Piper safely to us," Anna said. "What's in the envelope?"

Nigel opened it and out spilled a cell phone and a note like the last one, still demanding the money. He laid the contents on the table. The phone was one of those cheap pay-as-you-go models.

"So he's going to call you on this phone and tell you where to go once you are at the ruins."

"Yes," Nigel said. "He also said to come alone. I don't think he's going to allow Justine near me."

"We won't be physically with you. We're going to need a supersmall earpiece," Justine said. "Something that can't be seen. Also, as a backup, I think he should swallow a tracker. That way, we'll be able to keep an eye on him no matter what happens. Embedding one in your skin would leave a scar, since we'd have to do it today. And I'm pretty sure he'd check the phone to make sure we didn't put a tracking device in it. But we may as well try."

"I'll do it. I have the money in my account in Peru. He's going to give me an account to transfer the funds into," Nigel said.

"Does he say why he's doing this?" Anna asked.

"Not in his note. I know we weren't on the best of terms when he left."

"I thought the HR department handled all firings," Justine said.

"Normally they do, but when an employee is at upper-level management like Marshall was, I like to handle it myself."

"I'd say it was admirable, but not in this case," Anna said. "I'm going to keep this information to myself and see what Emile reveals to me. I get the feeling he's the one in charge of guarding Piper."

"Tell him I'll give him the two million Marshall is asking for if he brings her to me unharmed."

"I don't think—

"It's not up to Justine. This is what I want to do, Anna. Let him know."

"Okay. Is there someplace where I can grab a shower? We can meet back here in about forty-five minutes. I'll have the GPS tracker for Nigel. Justine, will that give you enough time to gather weapons and decide what we all should carry?"

"Yeah, that'll be fine," Justine said.

He took Anna down the hall to show her where the shower was. When he was about to leave, she stopped him.

"Don't mess around with Justine, Nigel."

"Mess around how?"

"By playing with her when you plan to walk away. She's not like other woman. She doesn't date or play the field."

"I'm sure she'd love that you are telling me this."

"She'll probably deck me, but I want you to know that if you hurt her, I'm coming after you and there won't be any place for you to hide."

Nigel nodded. "I'm not planning on hurting her."

"Good. Emile sent a message to me from Piper for you. She said to tell you that she was just like Justine . . . a warrior fairy."

Nigel smiled, imagining Piper saying that. He knew what she meant by it. She was ready to defend herself, and would escape the first chance she got.

"Give her a message from me. Tell her that I'm coming to get her and to stay put until she sees me."

"You think she'll run before the drop tonight?" Anna asked.

"If she sees a chance to escape, she'll try it."

"That would be so dangerous," Anna said, "but I understand why she'd do it."

"You do?"

"I was kidnapped when I was fourteen. So I really do understand what she's going through."

"When we get her back, will you talk to her about your experiences?" Nigel asked.

"If she wants me to, then, yes, I will."

"Thank you, Anna."

"Anytime, Nigel."

He walked back down the hall and found Justine standing over the table, rereading the notes. "Did you and Anna have a nice chat?"

"I guess. She warned me about not messing around with you."

"Did she? I don't need anyone to watch my back, Nigel."

"I know that. I think Anna does, too. She just wanted me to know that no matter how much of a loner you are . . . there are people who care about you."

Justine was seriously going to talk to Anna when they got back to the office about keeping her nose to herself. The woman should know better than to talk about her.

She went out to the Humvee and brought in two black bags that were bigger than she was. She'd always used them to carry her arsenal. She liked to be prepared, and she was the one on the team in charge of weapons.

Nigel wasn't in the main living area when she came back in, but she'd watched the front door and had a view of the side, so she suspected he was still in the house.

"Nigel?"

He walked out of the den and waved at her, signaling he was on the phone. She nodded at him and then went to work, assembling the weapons they'd need for the coming night.

It was a job she could do with her eyes shut, so that left her mind free to wander. One thought kept circling in her head: what Nigel had said about people caring about her.

That was the one thing she really couldn't tolerate . . . well, okay, she had more than one thing she couldn't tolerate, but she really didn't feel comfortable with emotion like that.

If Anna and Charity cared about her, then that left them vulnerable and it left her vulnerable, too. Emotions were a weakness that was really hard to protect against.

"Did you need me?" Nigel asked as he entered the room.

"No. I just wanted to make sure you were still in the house. I've been running around gathering weapons. I'm staying here, though. I figure the best chance we have of getting Piper back is the plan you guys came up with."

"Am I getting a weapon?"

"I think you should take yours with you. But nothing else. He's probably going to take it from you when you meet him face-to-face."

"I would," Nigel said. "So I'll be weaponless."

"I could show you a few moves . . . are you any good at punching?"

"I guess. Most people don't punch each other."

"I guess in your world, maybe. But if you are fighting for your life, you can punch him in the throat or in the groin."

Nigel moaned at that thought.

"I know guys hate to think about hitting that area, but if you are fighting for your life, there's no such thing as pride or looking cool."

"I know that."

"How are you with a knife?"

"I've never killed with one, or had a fight with one."

"Do you want one? I have a switchblade and sheath you could put on your arm. It's light, but deadly."

"I'll take it."

"The important thing to remember tonight—

"Why are you talking nonstop?"

"Because I want you to be prepared. We're going to do

everything we can to ensure that you are safe, and that we're there at the drop, but anything could happen. If you are left alone, you need to be prepared to save yourself—and Piper."

He drew her close and kissed her. He didn't hesitate or lead up to a deeper embrace, he just full-out kissed her, the way a man kisses his woman when he can't find the words to tell her how much she means to him.

Justine held on to his shoulders and kissed him back. Tried to show him how much he meant to her, and that for the first time, she was worried about going into a fight. Not for herself— she was like the cockroach that could survive anything—but she was scared for Nigel because he had a lot to lose, and losing Piper would break him.

Breaking him was something she really wanted to avoid because she wanted Nigel in one piece, happy and healthy. She held his head to hers and went up on her tiptoes to kiss him even more deeply. She took a breath and then stepped back.

"You have to be safe, Nigel."

"I will be. I have the very best bodyguard in the business."

"I'm serious."

"I know that, but I can't start worrying or I'll lose it."

She nodded. "Good, you be light and funny and crack jokes if that keeps you loose."

"Sex would help me wind down, but it doesn't seem to have the same effect on you."

She was ashamed that it didn't. But sharing her body with Nigel just made her tense, and made her struggle inside with the two women she was. One of the women had been hidden away so long she hadn't even realized there was more to Justine O'Neill than a tough-as-nails gal.

"What relaxes you?" Nigel asked, tucking a strand of hair behind her ear before he wrapped an arm around her shoulder and pulled her close to his side.

She stood there for a moment with him pressed so close against her and thought that maybe this was something that relaxed her, but then she felt her body changing. Her breasts felt full and heavy and her mind turned to thoughts of sex.

She pulled away from Nigel, and walked toward the table with the weapons on it. She needed to be the cool RoboCop girl she'd always been. Emotionless.

But she had the feeling that her emotions weren't going to just disappear the way she wanted them to. "Working the guns and making sure that they are all ready for us. I'll clean your gun, too, if you'd like."

"How about if I clean it, and keep you company?" Nigel suggested.

Justine nodded and watched him walk away. She knew she was going to have to let him go. She couldn't do her job and be in love with him.

Oh, no. She was in love with Nigel Carter. She'd never expected to fall in love, and she had no idea how to handle it now. So she did what she always did with her emotions: she shoved them way down low, out of the way. She'd just pretend it hadn't happened, and that she didn't know she'd fallen for Nigel.

Justine disappeared into the bedroom and came back out as the woman he'd first met. Black jeans, black T-shirt, and a pair of black leather boots. He knew she was armed to the teeth, and to be honest, she looked sexy as hell.

She was one lethal weapon. And the vulnerable woman he'd made love to earlier was completely gone. This woman was liable to bite his head off if he tried to touch her.

He felt a lot better knowing she was at his back. He'd made the decision to hire Liberty Investigations on the fly, but it was one of the best ones he'd made in years.

He was wearing a nearly invisible earpiece/microphone combo that would pick up his conversations and enable him to hear Justine, Anna, and Charity.

He also had swallowed a GPS tracking device, and according to Anna it was working right now. He had one embedded in the sole of his shoe and another one in the phone Marshall had sent.

There had been no further messages from Emile, and he could only hope that they'd go to the drop and Marshall would be happy with the money, but a part of Nigel knew the man wasn't going to let him walk away. He knew that Marshall had taken Piper because he wanted Nigel. And there was only one person in the world that Nigel would come after.

"You can take the Humvee. I will follow you on the motorcycle. Anna will be mobile, but hanging back to monitor communications and track all signals. Charity's going to be on another Dyna Rider, and she and I will change off following you."

"Okay. What if you lose me?"

"We don't intend to let that happen, but if it does, then remember what I told you. Fight for your life and your daughter's life. There is no such thing as pride in this kind of situation," Justine said.

"If I do lose contact, I will make my way back here," Nigel said.

"We'll meet you here." Justine said. She'd already disseminated the weapons and everyone had at least two semiautomatic guns and enough clips to keep them shooting until dawn, and whatever other weapons she could fit on the portable arsenal.

"Charity is going first, so she can already be in place at the ruins. Anna will be next. And then I'll head out when you do."

Anna had Charity's motorcycle loaded in the Humvee she

was driving, and would unload it off-road, away from the factory in case someone was watching them for Marshall. If Marshall had an inside man at Baron, then they might be screwed anyway. But Nigel didn't worry about that. They had contingency plans, and as long as he got Piper back, he'd be fine. He could handle whatever came at him if he knew Piper was safe.

They left the house on time and Justine was strangely quiet. "What are you thinking about?"

"Everything that we're dealing with. Don't forget—

"I know, Justine. I'm not going to forget anything. I promise."

"I wish I'd taken the time to teach Piper some moves. I've already recommended to Sam that if we take a child from now on, that we give them a class in basic self-defense."

"That's a good idea, but most clients are going to feel like they don't need to know how to defend themselves when they have your group."

"Why would someone put their own child in jeopardy? I couldn't work with someone who was too stupid to listen to what we advise them."

"Like me?"

She looked at him all serious for a minute. "Just like you. Central and South America are dangerous places for American children. You don't have to be über wealthy to be a target either."

"Believe me, I know that now."

"Maybe we could have you talk to the people who don't want to listen to us about their kids."

"Justine?"

"Yes, Nigel?"

He loved the sound of his name on her lips. There was something about hearing her call his name that made the bond between them seem stronger: He wanted to put her someplace safe, wanted to protect her so he didn't have to worry over her while he rescued his daughter.

It didn't matter to him that she was strong and capable. His instincts shouted for him to be the one to protect her.

"Be careful tonight. Don't forget to take all the advice you gave me."

She nodded. "I'm a survivor, Nigel. Don't worry about me. No matter how bad things look, I can always bounce back."

"Just be safe. I don't like seeing you shot at." He didn't say it out loud, but having just found Justine, he wasn't ready to lose her. She had made him realize that living for his job and his daughter wasn't enough to satisfy the man he was inside.

"Me, either," she said. "But that was really more like a graze."

Nigel pulled off the road onto the shoulder when she directed him to, and she got her motorcycle out of the back. He helped her get it down and then stood back while she climbed on. If anything went wrong tonight, this could be the last time he saw her. And that hurt. He wasn't nearly ready to say goodbye yet.

He leaned forward and kissed her. She closed her eyes and kissed him back for a moment, then pulled away.

"Justine, love, thank you for the last two days. They could have been hell for me and you made them bearable. No matter what happens tonight, please know that the blame rests solely with me."

She shook her head and put on her sunglasses. "If there is any blame, it's mine. You hired us to protect you and your daughter. And don't think that you won't see me again, Nigel. Men who think they aren't coming home don't come home."

And he needed to come back because he'd just discovered what had been missing in his life up until now. And that was Justine. She was the link that he and Piper had always known wasn't there, but had no idea how to replace.

He took her face in his hands and kissed her again. He

thrust his tongue deep into her mouth and let his hands skim down her body. She was a warrior and had on the armor of one. He felt the Kevlar vest instead of her breasts and at the curve of her waist was a gun belt.

But she kissed him like she was all woman. All his woman, he thought. And he wished he had time to make love to her again.

He wanted to go into this battle secure in the knowledge that she was his.

She turned on the bike and revved the engine. She mouthed something, then turned her head and checked the traffic before driving away. He got back into the Humvee, trying to figure out if what he thought he heard her say was what she actually said. He wasn't sure, but he thought that Justine had admitted to loving him. And that was all he needed to go get Piper. He knew that at the end of this night, he was going to sit down with Justine and find out exactly how she felt about him, because he knew he loved her, too.

Chapter Seventeen

Justine didn't question anything as she fell into position behind Nigel. This was the third stop he'd made in trying to get to Piper. She could hear the frustration in his voice with each consecutive stop they made. This time, he'd been directed back toward the jungle and a restaurant a half mile out of Cusco.

If Nigel had any kind of altitude problems, the running around was going to fatigue him. Luckily, she thought he was doing fine.

"I'm three cars back, Nigel," Justine said.

"If Marshall doesn't show up soon, I'm really going to lose my patience," he said.

"I know," Justine said.

This was the hard part of negotiating with criminals. They had to play games like this in order to keep from being caught. "Charity is going to pick you up again after this stop."

"Any word from Emile?"

"Nothing yet."

"The place is up ahead. It's closed for remodeling," Nigel said.

"I'm going to go past you and double back. Be safe."

"I will be."

She watched the Humvee pull off the road into the parking lot, which only had a few cars in it. She kept her eyes on the road and drove past on the motorcycle. This was the part of her job she really didn't like. She could take risks all day long and it didn't bother her, but watching someone else put their life on the line . . . she didn't like that.

She pulled off the road when she heard Nigel enter the restaurant. She left the bike parked in the jungle where it wasn't visible from the street.

"Search him," a man said.

"I hardly think searching me is going to help, Marshall," Nigel said. "I've got a gun and that's all."

"I doubt that. I know you have a bodyguard."

"How do you know that?"

"I may have mentioned it," Alfred said, his accented voice strong and clear as it came over the microphone.

She heard the sounds of Nigel being patted down. They found the gun and the knife she'd given him to put at the small of his back. But they didn't take the earpiece.

"I want to see my daughter, and then we can use this phone to wire the money to you."

"I'm in charge now, Nigel. You don't call the shots. I do."

"Fine," he said, his accent crisp and a bit cold. "But let's get it over with. I'm tired of chasing you all over this city."

"Are you tired? Maybe now I don't seem so incompetent."

"No, you still do."

She heard the sound of a fist connecting with flesh and guessed that Nigel had taken a punch. She heard him spit, probably blood. "My daughter."

"You'll see her when I'm ready for you to. Take him down the hall and remove every bit of clothing. Liberty Investigations has a reputation for being very thorough. I bet he has a tracking device on him."

Justine heard nothing but footsteps and knew Anna and Charity would be silent while Nigel was being searched. She pulled her BlackBerry from her pocket and sent a text message to the other woman.

<Justine>: I'm a half mile north of Nigel. Working my way back toward him.
<Charity>: I have the building in my sight. And am set up for a sniper shot.
<Anna>: Let's get Nigel and Piper out first. I'm still getting a strong signal from Nigel.
<Justine>: I'm moving in. Anna, do you have any plans on the building?
<Anna>: The east side seems to be the place where they are doing the construction. Come in that way.
<Charity>: I'll cover you.
<Justine>: Be right there.

She moved through the brush and jungle-like terrain. She knew from past experience that the plants in the jungle could be more dangerous than the animals, though she did keep her eye out for spiders, which were very poisonous here.

"Take off all your clothes," Alfred ordered Nigel.

"Listen, I am a wealthy man. I can make it worth your while to work for me instead of Marshall."

"Marshall owns the land my family lives on. You can't give me back my home, can you?"

"I can give you a nice new home. Whatever home you want in the Baron compound."

"No. I'm not interested in that. Marshall knows you too well. He said you would offer me a bribe. When you have your clothes off, put on those over here."

She heard the sounds of disrobing and knew Nigel was following orders and getting dressed again. "I have to bind your hands now. Then we will go back."

She was surprised Alfred hadn't notice the switchblade and she wondered how Nigel had hidden it from the security guard.

"Okay, now you will ride in my car to the final destination. You will have to walk a bit. I'm sorry that your shoes have to be left behind, but I've heard there are devices that can be embedded in them."

"If you'd shown this much initiative at work, you'd still have a job."

"I didn't like my work at Baron, but this job I think I'll keep."

"Kidnapping and extortion? That's a pretty risk line of business."

"Not really. Executives always pay to keep their families safe."

Justine realized that this wasn't the first time Marshall had done something like this. And it made an odd kind of sense. The mercenaries they'd battled at his compound were expensive and well paid, and the only way he could have that kind of cash flow was to be in an illegal trade.

Nigel didn't give a damn where Marshall took him. He was tired of being dragged from place to place, and was ready to do more than exchange words with Marshall. Clearly the man had found work after he'd left Baron Industries, and he had a feeling that he wasn't using linkedin.com for job hunting, but more for executive hunting, to find information on people he then targeted for kidnapping and extortion.

They left the restaurant, and Nigel felt pretty good about the fact that at least the earpiece and GPS tracker were still on him.

Marshall hardly resembled the senior manager he'd seen every day in white dress shirts and ties. He looked very at home in the jungle, with his fatigues on and his weapon strapped to his thigh.

"Why not drug running?"

"My cousin is in that line of work, and I'm not interested in competing against him."

Baron really needed a much better system to vet their employees. Why had they never realized that Marshall had all of these connections?

"Your daughter is being held in one of the jungle villages of my cousins. I will give you the name of the village, and the direction it is located in, once the money has been transferred into my account."

"I'm not giving you any money until Piper is with me. So why don't you call your cousin and tell him to bring my daughter to me."

"You aren't the boss anymore, Nigel. I am."

"I can't pay you until I know Piper is alive."

"I thought you'd say that. I have a phone and you can talk to her."

Marshall went to the other side of the room and dialed a number on an old satellite phone that was big and definitely out of date. But it still worked.

"Let me speak to Emile."

So Emile was still with Piper, but that didn't mean it was good news for them. Emile had sold them out once, and might still do so again.

"Put the girl on the phone," Marshall said.

"Hello, Piper. Would you like to speak to your father?"

Marshall held the phone to Nigel's ear. "Piper?"

Static crackled over the line and he heard a voice say "Daddy," but it was so distorted he had no idea if it was Piper or not.

"Piper, is that you?"

Again, mainly static and the thread of a voice.

He pulled his head back from the phone. "I can't distinguish if that is my daughter."

Marshall hung up the phone. "You can't even recognize your own kid. What does that say about you?"

"I think it says that you don't have my kid. So you either produce her or I'm walking."

Nigel started for the door and heard Marshall following him. "If you walk out of here, you'll never see her again."

"I'm guessing you want the money. You know I'm willing to deal, but I have to see her and know she's alive."

Marshall nodded. "Very well. I will take you to her, but it will cost you an extra half million dollars."

"Sure, fine. Let's go."

The vehicle he was led to had darkened windows and large all-terrain tires. It was a sturdy vehicle.

Nigel looked at the driver, trying to see if it was Emile, but the man wasn't. He took heart from the fact that Piper was probably safe with the mercenary.

He was shoved to the backseat of the vehicle, and hit the bruised side of his face as he landed. He grunted in pain and then sat up. When he did, he noticed the earpiece had fallen out and was now on the seat. He sat down near it and used his fingers to pick it up.

Since his hands were bound behind his back, he couldn't put the piece back in his ear. All he could do was hold it so they could hear the conversation.

The jeep bounced over the rough road and up the mountain path. They followed the road until it met a stream, and then they were forced to stop.

"We have to walk from here," Marshall said.

Nigel knew this was going to be tough. But he didn't say anything or complain as they started walking. It was hard to keep his balance on the jungle trail, especially with his hands bound behind his back. But he didn't care about anything. He just kept focused on the fact that Piper was in some village up here, and he was going to see her soon. He hoped like hell that Justine was still on his trail, because he knew he was going to need reinforcements.

He stumbled over a root and tumbled to the ground. The fall jarred him and he dropped the earpiece. He tried to pick it back up, but was dragged to his feet before he could get it.

The terrain in the jungle was rough, and Justine and Charity were as close behind Nigel as they could be. Anna was almost with them, but they weren't waiting for her, knowing that time was of the essence. They were pretty sure Nigel had lost his earpiece because they had lost track of his conversations a few minutes ago.

"I hate the jungle," Charity said.

"I don't mind it too much," Justine said. They were both running at a steady but slow pace. They had no other choice because the trail they were on wasn't the best. The signal from Nigel's GPS tracker kept going in and out.

Justine kept her BlackBerry in one hand, with the tracker application opened. "This bites. I keep losing him every few minutes."

"Do you have a consistent signal, Anna?"

"Yes. Do you want me to stay here by the vehicles? They'll have to come out this way."

"Yes. That's a good idea. Let us know when they stop."

"I will. Right now, you two aren't too far behind them. I think the best thing to do would be to get within five hunded feet and keep that pace," Charity said.

"Okay. I'll let you know when you are that close," Anna said.

"So what's up with you and Nigel?"

"Now?"

"You know you'd never talk to me if we weren't trapped here together. And since we're trekking through the jungle . . . "

"There's nothing. He's our client, and I'm doing my job."

Something whizzed past her ear and Justine dove for the ground at the same time Charity did. They both rolled into the underbrush on opposite sides of the path. "Someone is shooting at us," Justine said.

"It's not Nigel," Anna said.

"I'm going to return fire," Justine said, drawing her weapon. She'd brought her silencer because sound carried, and sometimes it was better in these situations to be as quiet as possible.

She rolled over on her stomach and scanned the horizon, looking for anything out of the ordinary. She noticed a leaf twitching, like something had bumped against it. The entire jungle got silent and she knew there was someone not too far from them. Someone who had spooked the animals and insects into hiding.

"I think our guy is ahead to the left."

"Take your shot when ready," Charity said.

Justine took a deep breath and waited until she saw that leaf move again. And then pulled the trigger and fired. She heard the ping of the bullet being fired through the silencer and then a faint grunt.

She'd hit someone.

She fired again in the same vicinity and someone returned fire. Justine eased forward on her stomach, staying low, trying carefully to stay out of any poisonous plants.

She saw a print of a boot to the left, and heard the footstep a minute before the man came out on the path. She shot him at close range in the thigh, and he dropped to one knee. She sprang to her feet and he came at her with a knife, slicing up toward her right arm.

"Get down," Charity said in her ear, and Justine dove to the left as Charity fired and hit the man between the eyes. He fell forward—dead.

"We're going to need a body bag, Anna. Do you have a lock on my position?"

"Yes. I'll send the authorities when we do cleanup."

Justine walked back to Charity and didn't say anything. Why hadn't she taken the shot and killed that man when she'd had the chance? She never hesitated to kill. Was this what loving Nigel had done to her? Had it made her so she was afraid to do her job?

But she hadn't minded causing him injury. She had simply not wanted to take a life.

"He wasn't going down easy," Charity said.

Justine had had her fill of killing last night at the compound. She'd been angry and had seen that killing rage in Nigel. And coming on top of finding Constance, it had been too much. "I always take the shot. Why didn't I this time?"

"I have no idea. But a little girl's life is danger. Maybe you were thinking that questioning that man would be better than killing him."

"Maybe. Or it could be that I'm changing. Did what happen to you and Daniel change you?"

"What happened? Do you mean falling in love with him?"

"Yes."

"Why, do you think you're in love with Nigel?"

"Never mind. Why did I even bring this up? Let's just stay on the path. I think it's safe to assume Marshall has someone guarding his back trail."

"I think so."

They continued down the path a little farther, and Justine tried not to think too much about what had happened and about how she'd hesitated, but she couldn't help it. She was changing, whether she wanted to admit it or not, and there was nothing she could do to change it.

"Um, yeah, I did change when Daniel came into my life. It was like all the stuff I didn't really like about myself—being with him made it right.

"Really?"

"Yes. Does that help you?"

Justine shrugged. She knew that Charity wasn't just a pretty face. That she had a lost her parents when she was young, and that had made her into the woman she was today. But she didn't have a murder in her past the way Justine did.

Was she really trying to think about a future with Nigel? That was completely crazy. She forced herself to pay attention to the trail, and didn't think about anything other than when she saw a target, she needed to take the shot.

"I like Nigel. I think he's a smart man, and if he's the right guy for you, it'll work out."

"What if he only wants me because of this situation? Everything is more intense right now because his daughter's life is in danger."

"I don't know," Charity said. "I worried about the same thing with Daniel."

"Daniel was totally smitten with you."

"Maybe from your vantage point. It's different when you're the one going through all those emotions," Charity said.

"Really? You seem like the kind of woman who can handle any man. . . . I mean, you've been engaged before."

"Yes, I have. But those other men were different. They didn't bother to see the real me."

Charity stopped walking and Justine did, too. "I guess what I'm trying to say is that when you meet a man during this kind of a mission, they have no choice but to see the real you. There's no illusion about the type of woman you are."

She had a point. And Justine didn't dwell on it anymore. One of the things she'd learned fairly early in her life was that she couldn't change anyone else, or their decisions. The question she needed to answer was if what she felt for Nigel was real, or if it was only something spurred on by the situation.

"Anna, are we getting close?"

"Not yet, but they've stopped moving."

Charity looked at her and they both started running again. In her head, Justine heard the music of AC/DC's "Back in Black," which always got her pumped up, and she roared it in her mind to drown out the sounds of Nigel and Piper's voices.

Because she knew time was of the essence now, and she couldn't afford to lose either one of them.

She stumbled as she realized that falling in love was the scariest thing she'd ever experienced. She'd thought she was self-contained and safe from harm because she'd walked away from her family, and the only people she'd cared about were Charity and Anna, who could protect themselves better than anyone Justine knew.

But she hadn't protected herself, hadn't learned any survival instincts. Instead, she'd simply been hiding from her emotions, and now that they were out in the open, she had no idea how to control them.

Chapter Eighteen

The village they entered was primitive by American standards, but had all the modern conveniences. He saw electricity lines running into the houses. In the middle of the village was a common area where children and women were gathered.

Everyone stopped when they saw Marshall. Dusk was falling, but it wasn't completely dark. Nigel felt awkward with his hands bound behind his back, along with the open wound on his cheek. His arms ached, and he was tired and worried and needed to see Piper. Then he wanted to get the hell out of Peru. He was still going to open the Baron factory here because he refused to let Marshall win, but he wouldn't be coming down here to oversee it.

Marshall shoved him toward a stump. "Sit there."

Nigel was happy to get off his aching feet. They were bloodied and cut up from the walk. He'd tried to stay on the trail, but had fallen more than once on the uneven terrain.

He saw Emile from across the village square. The man seemed to nod toward him, and then disappeared.

He wished to hell he knew what that meant. About ten minutes later, Marshall went into the largest house in the village. Nigel tried to stand, but couldn't. He rolled to his side on the ground and got his knees beneath him. Slowly he stood, rising to his knees one at a time.

He almost cursed out loud at the pain in his feet. They were cut and swollen and hurt like the devil. He looked around the area, searching for something to use to cut the flex cuffs at his wrists.

He saw a corrugated building on the outskirts and slowly, keeping to the shadows, he moved toward the building. He felt around the edge until he found one sharp enough he hoped would be able to cut the cuffs.

He worked the cuffs up and down and he thought of what Justine had warned him of. That there was no room for pride in life-or-death situations.

His wrist was being scraped raw, but he didn't care. He kept working slowly and steadily. He couldn't wait for Justine to come to the rescue. That went against the grain, to wait for that anyway. He felt the tension on his wrists lessen and then give way. He pulled his hands free.

His shoulders ached as he rotated them, and then he rubbed his wrists. He knew he should cover any open wounds. The jungle was a breeding ground for disease.

But he wanted to find Piper. He heard the villagers all talking at once and realized they had noticed he wasn't in his spot anymore. He debated in that split second going back over there, but decided to search for Piper. He was unarmed, but he could fight dirty, and he'd find a weapon while he was searching for her.

He started with the house nearest him. There was no one inside, but he found an old machete. The handle was aged, but the blade was clean, and when he tested it, he found it was very sharp.

He tucked the machete into his waistband where he could reach it easily. He went to the next building and peered into one of the windows. It was a one-room house that held a bed against one wall, and a kitchen table. Otherwise, it was deserted. He wondered if everyone was in the common area at this time of the day.

He heard footsteps behind him and kept moving in a circle to the right. Staying still wasn't going to help anything. He ducked around the corner of the house he'd just searched and drew the machete.

He heard the footsteps again, and held his breath, waiting. He saw no movement but sensed that someone was there. He put his arm out in the dark and jerked the person back against him. He brought the long blade of the machete up under the person's chin.

"It's me," Justine said.

He relaxed his hold on her and she turned in his arms. "There's no time. Piper is being held in one of these houses. Will you help me search?"

"Of course I will," she said.

He hugged her close before letting go. "Thank God you are here."

"Charity is working her way in from the other direction," Justine said. They both moved off in the same direction. She handed him a gun and a clip. "Not that the machete isn't effective."

"Thanks," he said. "I saw Emile. He nodded at me, but that was it."

"Anna hasn't heard from him, and I'm not sure how far we can trust him."

"I lost the earpiece. I'm sorry about that."

"It's not a problem," she said. "We are here, and we aren't going to let Marshall leave."

"Alfred is working for him," Nigel warned. He was a little lightheaded from all the blood he'd lost, and he knew he wasn't as coherent as he could be.

"We heard."

"I'm firing him. And I want everyone on my staff to—

"Nigel. Look at me."

"Why?"

"You are rambling. Are you okay?"

"I think so. My feet are swollen and I think I may have stepped on some kind of stinging insect."

"Anna? Do I have an EpiPen?"

Nigel couldn't hear Anna's answer, but a few minutes later, Justine pulled a pen from her pocket and stabbed him with it. Immediately he felt the swelling in his feet recede.

"I think you were having a reaction," Justine said.

"I think so, too. I'm feeling better now."

"I don't suppose I could convince you to sit here and wait for me to get back with Piper."

"Not on your life. If you need to go back to Anna, you can leave."

Justine looked up at him with those steely eyes of hers, in that sweet pixie face, and shook her head. "I'm not leaving until you do."

Justine couldn't imagine them in worse shape. Nigel had stopped rambling and his color had returned, but she knew he wasn't up to his full strength yet. Charity was finding the same thing, that most of the huts were deserted. The people of the village had fanned out and were searching the jungle area, looking for Nigel, she supposed.

They met up with Charity in the middle of the village near the large house. "That's where Marshall went."

"How many people are inside?"

"I saw two people go in when he did."

"Anna?"

"Yes?"

"Can you get a thermal image of the village for us?" Justine asked. "We need to know how many people are in the large house in the center of the village."

"I'm on it."

Justine waited and noted how anxious Nigel was beside her. She knew he couldn't wait another minute to get to his daughter. She was amazed that he'd freed himself and started searching. "Why didn't Marshall put a guard on you?"

"Because I knew he wouldn't go far without his daughter," Marshall answered her. "Put your hands on your head and turn to face me."

Justine did as she was ordered. Marshall wasn't that tall, and there was a weakness around his eyes that reminded her a lot of Franklin Baron. He seemed like a little bully of a man.

"What are you staring at?"

"You," she said.

"Like what you see?"

"No. Two-bit criminals aren't my cup of tea."

He backhanded her, knocking her off balance and into Nigel, who caught her.

"Keep your hands to yourself," Nigel said.

Justine realized Charity had blended into the shadows when Marshall had captured her and Nigel.

"Where is the girl?" she asked as Alfred came up behind her. He bound her hands behind her back, but left all of her weapons on her. She realized he was either stupid or didn't care enough about Marshall to want the other man to win.

"Inside. Are you ready to wire my money?" Marshall asked Nigel.

"As soon as I have my daughter."

"Then let's go inside so we can finish our business. Alfred, bring the woman."

Justine allowed herself to be manhandled up the steps and into the house. Nigel ran across the room to the pallet on the floor where Piper lay curled on her side. She seemed unharmed from her position across the room, but was unconscious, and her lips were cracked as if she was dehydrated.

Marshall walked over to Nigel and jerked him to his feet. "You've seen the girl. Now do your part. I need that money wired into my account."

"I am going to need a guarantee of safe passage out of here— for me, Piper, and Justine."

"No more negotiating. The deal was your daughter for the money. Now call."

He handed a cell phone to Nigel. He took the device from Marshall and held it loosely in his left hand. Justine was not a bit surprised that Nigel had renewed strength now that they were here with Piper. It seemed to her that seeing his daughter had reenergized him. Made him realize he couldn't give up.

"I can't remember the number," Nigel said.

Marshall balled his hand and raised it toward Nigel, who just stood his ground, staring at the other man. From across the room, Justine could feel the disdain that Nigel had for Marshall.

Marshall lowered his hand and pulled a Remington semiautomatic weapon from the holster at his side. He pointed the weapon at Piper. "Call or she dies. I'm not bluffing, Nigel. You have less than a minute to dial the number."

Nigel moved his fingers over the keys on the phone. Both men were balancing on a tightrope. They both had something the other wanted, but giving in too soon would spell destruction for either one of them.

"I'm coming in from the left," Charity said. Justine heard her in the earpiece and knew she needed to stop Charity from startling Marshall.

"Stop," she said.

"Me?" Charity asked in her ear.

"Shut up, bitch. Your life isn't necessary here."

"No, you shut up," Justine said, lowering her shoulder and driving her body into Alfred. Her move startled the guard and knocked him off balance. She kept driving until she got him completely on the ground. She used pressure from her foot on his windpipe to knock him out. Then turned to face Marshall, who was coming toward her.

He fired at her, but she dove for the ground, rolling as best she could with her hands behind her back. Nigel had crossed the room to Piper and had his daughter in his arms.

"Charity, northwest window, now."

"I'm there."

Justine struggled to her feet, watching as Marshall came closer to her. Nigel had his sights on the window, and as soon as he turned his back on them to lower Piper through the opening, Marshall turned and fired two shots at Nigel's back.

She saw them hit him, and watched as he shook and fell forward. Justine was in motion even as Marshall turned toward her. She jumped a few feet away from him, using a flying sidekick aimed at his shoulder. He fired the gun and she felt the bullet impact on the same thigh where she already had a wound. But her kick was on target, and it took him down.

Charity came in through the open window and coldcocked Marshall on the side of the head, knocking him out. Justine left Marshall to Charity, then went to Nigel. She had to climb through the window to get to him.

"I'm okay," he said. He was holding his daughter in his arms, and she thought that maybe at last he would be okay. Having Piper with him was what he needed.

The bullet in her thigh was throbbing, and she heard a faint buzzing sound before she started to sway.

"Oh, damn, I'm going to pass out," she said, and then the world went black.

* * *

Justine awoke to smelling salts being waved under her nose. She jerked upright, feeling a wave of pain in her thigh.

Charity had one hand on her shoulder. "Where are you hurt?"

"Thigh. Bullet wound . . . not a graze this time."

"Can you walk out, or do you want me to have Anna send someone down to get you?"

"I can walk," Justine said. "Where's Nigel?"

"Over there with Emile. He's the one who got all the villagers away from here so that we'd only have to deal with Alfred and Marshall."

"Well, I guess that's something."

Charity shrugged.

"Do you need a hand?"

Justine hated to admit it, but she did. She took the hand that Charity offered and got to her feet.

"Do you need me here?"

"No. Why don't you lead Nigel and Piper out of here?" Charity suggested.

"I will."

She made her way over to them and Nigel looked up at her. "Piper hasn't woken up yet."

"Did Charity find out what he was using to sedate Piper?"

"According to Emile, it was just an over-the-counter type of thing. The effects should wear off in the next two to three hours."

"Are you ready to go back to the vehicles? Anna will have a medical professional waiting for us."

"Can you walk out?"

"Yes. I'm fine. How's your back? I saw you take those two bullets."

"Sore," he said.

Justine realized that for all the talk between them, there

was no real communication going on. Nigel was pushing her back into the role of stranger, and she was letting him.

When she'd seen Marshall shoot at him, she'd felt a panic well inside her that, to be honest, she hadn't been able to control. She knew better than to let herself care this deeply for anyone, and yet somehow Nigel had found his way into that small circle of people she cared about.

"Are we okay?" she asked Nigel.

"Yes. Of course we are. I just need to focus on Piper right now."

She understood that. She hoped he didn't think that she needed more attention than his daughter. What kind of selfish woman would she be?

With a man like Nigel, his daughter was always going to come first, and it was time she acknowledged that. She shook her head and realized it didn't bother her at all. Part of why she loved him was because of his dedication to his daughter.

"Let's get her to safety," Justine said. She led the way out of the village. A few of the villagers were returning as they left, and gave them a wide berth. Nigel looked battered and barely able to stand as he walked next to her.

Nigel took the lead when the jungle around them became denser. She followed him, watching the man she loved, and wondering how she was going to deal with him once they were out of this place.

"I'm surprised we haven't run into any tribes," Justine said. She'd noticed signs of people in the rain forest, but they had yet to encounter anyone. She thought that maybe they all had a live-and-let-live attitude, which worked for her.

Or maybe she should say, had worked for her. Because she wanted to figure out a way to still be herself and live with Nigel. But to be honest, she couldn't. In her head, she still pictured him in that perfect house with a well-coiffed wife.

"Me, too. But maybe the fact that Marshall has been keeping everyone in this area under his thumb has worked in our favor."

The Amazon Basin was filled with many different tribes. And like people everywhere, there were times when they were warring. Also, there were the gold miners who ventured into this area. They didn't like anyone who came near them.

"Do you want me to help carry Piper?" Justine asked. She wasn't sure she could carry Piper, but Nigel was limping from walking on his wounded feet, and she wanted to do something to help him.

"No. You have enough to worry about, keeping yourself upright."

"I know. We look like the losers." She felt like one, too. She was battered and aching, and she knew tomorrow she was going to feel even worse. She had to look like hell, but Nigel had never really seemed to be attracted to her because of her hair or her makeup.

"Looks can be deceiving," Nigel said.

"Yes, they can," she said. She'd never thought a man like Nigel—a Baron Industries executive—would be a man she could love. But he was.

It had been a rough day so far, and the night promised to be even longer. They still had a lot of work to do to wrap up everything that had happened in the jungle. There were arrests to be made, injuries to be treated, and as they moved back out of the jungle, she realized a distance was growing between her and Nigel.

Justine knew herself well enough to know that though Nigel seemed fascinating and different here in the Amazon Basin, once they returned to civilization, he'd be like all the other men she'd known, and lose interest in her.

Well, maybe not, but she'd be back to her old self. The woman who knew better than to trust any *man*.

"Are we really having this conversation?" he asked.

She knew what he meant. Maybe she was going a little crazy from everything that had happened. She knew it was inane, but it was the only thing that kept her from the fatigue that dogged her every step. That and the fear that rode shotgun with it. She couldn't close her eyes without being assailed with some image that was so foreign to her everyday life, that it made her feel like she was someone else.

"I'm tired," Justine said suddenly. Her wound continued to throb, and all she really wanted was to curl up in Nigel's arms. And that so wasn't like her.

Maybe that was part of the problem. For the first time, she was in a situation that she couldn't handle on her own. A situation she didn't want to handle on her own. God, she'd only known the man a little over a day. He didn't mean anything to her. Yet at the same time, he did.

He stood there, watching her. She felt a million things at once, but mostly she focused on the sense of urgency in the back of her mind, and the feeling that time was running out for her and Nigel.

And she still needed him. She had the strange feeling that a lifetime together wasn't going to be enough time to figure out this man.

And that scared her, because she had no idea if she had the stamina to spend a lifetime with Nigel. But her heart ached at the thought of not spending the rest of her life with him.

Chapter Nineteen

Nigel paid for the best for Piper. She'd been airlifted out of Cusco and flown straight to the best hospital in Lima. Justine had accompanied him because he'd flat-out refused to let her stay behind. She'd barely made the long trek out of the jungle, and had collapsed as soon as they'd met up with Anna.

Justine had needed to have the bullet removed from her thigh. She was out of surgery now, and in a recovery room right next to Piper's.

Nigel didn't know what the future held for he and Justine, but he knew that he wasn't going walk away from her.

"Daddy?"

"I'm here, Piper."

He went to her and bent low over her bed, brushing a kiss on her forehead. "I had a really bad dream."

"Well, I'm here now, and you are safe."

"Is Constance okay?" Piper asked, sitting up in bed, looking around the room for her nanny.

"Constance didn't make it out of the jungle, baby."

Tears fell down Piper's face. Nigel sat down beside her and drew her into his arms. "I miss her, Daddy."

"I know, Pip. I miss her, too."

She closed her eyes and he felt her body go limp against his as she drifted off to sleep.

"Daddy?" she asked, sleepily stirring in his arms.

"Hmm?"

"I want to go home," Piper said, looking up at him with those bright eyes of hers.

"We are going home as soon as the doctor says you can travel."

Piper drifted back to sleep. He'd had similar conversations with her each time she woke. There was always that moment of panic in her voice, and then her desire to go home.

Nigel just needed to take care of her. And he knew he'd never make the same mistakes he had before. Arrogantly thinking that he and Piper were safe as long as they were together. He stepped into the hallway and opened the door to Justine's room. She was resting quietly in her bed. He watched her from the door for a few moments, tempted to go inside and hold her. He'd needed that for so long, but he was afraid that now that they were both back in the real world, she was going to push him away.

Justine wasn't the type of woman who'd just let him take over her life. Anyone else, and he would have known that a proposal and some sweet words would win her over, but not Justine.

He saw her move restlessly in the bed, and walked into her room. He put his hand on her shoulder to calm her, that touch soothing him as he saw her relax. He bent low and brushed his lips over her forehead before walking out of her room and back into Piper's. As soon as he checked on his daughter, he went to the alcove and called Sam Liberty.

"Hello, Nigel."

"Sam, I need another bodyguard."

"The team assures me they got everyone who was threatening you."

"It's not for me. I need someone to help me watch over Piper and Justine until I can get them back to the States."

"Justine?"

"Yes. Is that a problem?"

"No. Not at all. I'll have to see if I have another team available. Anna and Charity are still finishing up the work at your factory in Cusco."

"That's fine. I just don't want to take any chances with either of them."

"Justine doesn't react well to coddling," Sam said.

"I understand that. I have another job for you as well."

"What kind of job?"

"Just a records search. It's a personal matter, Sam, and I'd appreciate your discretion on this one."

Sam took a deep breath. "You can trust me, Nigel. What is it you need?"

"I want the name of Justine's stepfather. She told me some things about her past, and I'm not sure if you are familiar with the details."

"I am," Sam said. "Nigel, that is a situation that is better left alone. She doesn't want anything from that life to touch the woman she is today."

Nigel knew that, but without resolving her past, Justine was a prisoner to it. And he thought maybe confronting the ghosts of her stepfather would help.

"So, you won't help me with this?"

"No. I can't."

"Very well. When will you know about the bodyguard?"

"In a few hours, probably. How should I reach you?" Sam asked.

Nigel looked at his watch and realized it was after ten. Much later than it seemed to him. "Text me and I'll call you back."

"Very good. Bye."

Nigel felt pretty good considering all the trauma his body had been through. That EpiPen had probably saved his life. The ER doctor had said that the poisonous plant he'd stepped on could have been deadly for someone with a reaction like his.

Justine had done so much for him. More than she'd probably ever realize. But she had saved his life in the jungle, and his sanity, when they'd been hunting for Piper. Without her, he wasn't sure he'd have made it through the last forty-eight hours.

How could he repay that?

He looked over at Piper, with her little stuffed bunny tucked close to her chin as she slept. The doctor he'd talked to had said that her memories would return over time, but not to worry because these types of traumas were best managed by being open and keeping the child safe.

Nigel knew that having the right people around Piper would help as well, and he also knew that he needed—no, he wanted—a woman like Justine to be an influence over Piper as well.

Justine woke in the middle of the night. She couldn't stand hospitals, and this one wasn't going to change her mind. She'd come to Lima with Nigel because she hadn't wanted to leave his side, but she hadn't planned on staying here.

She reached for her BlackBerry to check the time: two a.m. She had a message from Sam to call him back. None of her was sure what time zone Sam lived in, but whenever they called him, he always answered his phone.

"Hello, Justine."

"Hello, Sam. I'm returning your call."

"How are your injuries? Did the surgery go okay on your thigh?"

"Everything went well. The doctor said probably six weeks tops, and I'll be back to normal. I'm going to start working out on my thigh as soon as I can to keep the muscle strength. I don't want to lose any of it."

"Good. I need you in top shape if you're coming back."

Justine had to play that last part back in her mind. "Did you say, 'if'?"

"Yes. I had a conversation with Nigel earlier tonight."

"About?"

"Hiring a bodyguard to protect you."

"Like hell. And by the way, I am coming back to work. I'm nothing without my job."

Sam said nothing to her for a long moment, and she sat there digesting what he'd said and how she'd responded. She'd discovered another part of herself with Nigel, but that didn't mean she was ready to leave behind who she had been.

"I am not quitting, Sam."

"Good. I didn't think you were, but I had to ask . . . there's something else I need to talk to you about."

"Okay. What is it?"

"I'm not sure how to say this."

"Sam, you are never tongue-tied. Whatever it is, I'll get over being pissed at you."

"Ha. I didn't do anything to make you angry. Nigel asked me to do something private and personal for him, and it involved you."

"How?"

"He asked me to look into who your stepfather is."

"What did you say?" Justine knew that one word from Sam, and Nigel would probably run from her like the pariah she was, where respectable society was concerned.

"I advised him that you wouldn't appreciate him doing that."

Justine leaned back against the pillow on the hospital bed.

Her entire body ached from being shot at. She was tired, but she realized for the first time she was actually pretty close to being content with her life and where she was in it.

"He thinks . . . "

"What?"

"That the past shapes us into the person we are."

Sam cleared his throat. "I agree with that."

"I've always hidden my past and kept it buried. I don't really want anyone to know the girl I was."

Her hand itched where they'd put in an IV drip. She scratched around the tape, wondering if she should just pull it out and get out of this bed. She should leave this hospital room, and just walk out of this life.

"I could start again, and no one would even know the difference."

"I would know," Sam said, his deep voice a little gruffer than usual.

"Do you remember when we first met . . . ha, I mean when you first called me?

"Yes, I do. You thought I was a blackmailer."

"I did," Justine said. Back then she hadn't trusted anyone at all. She was more concerned with watching her own back, and had been confident that everyone she met would use the fact that she'd killed a man against her.

"You really helped change me, Sam. Made me into a better person. I'm not sure I've ever thanked you for that."

"You're welcome. Are you saying good-bye?"

Justine thought long and hard about that. Before she'd come to Peru with Nigel, she'd known something had to change in her life, but sitting here she realized she didn't want it to be her job.

"No, I'm not. Saving people is something I'm good at, and I can't imagine going back to being a vigilante."

"I'm glad to hear it," Sam said. "Can I give you a piece of advice?"

"When have you not?"

Sam laughed. "Tell Nigel everything so he doesn't find it out later."

"I have told him all of it."

"But not the name," Sam said and hung up.

Justine played with her BlackBerry, knowing she'd held out on the name because Nigel worked for the family who had betrayed her. Justine knew they all weren't bad people, but some of them had been, and she was afraid of his reaction if he did tell her about Franklin Baron.

It had been three days since Nigel and Piper were admitted to the hospital. Justine had left yesterday and was now resting comfortably at a private home owned by Liberty Investigations.

Nigel had a hired driver take them to Justine's address. There had been no time to really talk to her at the hospital. And there was still so much left unsaid between them.

And she'd left without saying a word. He knew that she'd been called back to talk to the officials about what had happened in the jungle, and to answer for the men she'd killed.

He knew that because he'd done the same thing in Piper's hospital room.

He and Piper got out of the car, and his daughter put her small hand in his. "Are you nervous, Daddy?"

"I am, Pip. I don't know why, though."

"I think it's because you like Justine, and miss her."

"Really?" he asked his daughter. "Why do you think that?"

"You keep staring at the sketch I did of her," Piper said.

"Do I?"

"Yes," she said.

"I do like her, Piper, and if there's a way, I want Justine to come and be part of our family."

"Like Constance was?"

"No. Like your mum was."

"Oh," Piper said, getting very quiet. He turned to his daughter and dropped down on one knee so they were eye level.

"What's the matter? Don't you like Justine?"

"I don't really know her," Piper said.

Nigel realized that over the last few days, his relationship had changed so much with Justine. But to Piper she was still just the bodyguard who looked like a fairy. "It wouldn't have to be right away."

Piper nodded. "I do like her, Daddy."

"This discussion could be for nothing. She might not like me enough to want to be a part of our family."

"Let's go inside and find out," Piper said.

He smiled a little at his daughter. She was getting her spirit back after the effects of the drugs left her system. She was still sad at bedtime, when she missed Constance, but Nigel thought with time that would pass, too.

They rang the bell and a few moments later Charity answered the door.

"I'm here to see Justine," Nigel said, by way of a greeting.

"Come in," she said. "Hello, Piper, how are you feeling?"

"Pretty good today, thank you."

Charity led them into a main living area that was furnished with oversized stuffed couches. "There's a portrait gallery down the hall, Piper. Would you like to see it?"

She nodded. "Is that okay, Daddy?"

"Sure. Where is Justine?"

"Outside in the gardens."

He walked toward the French doors that led outside, and stood on the terrace for a few minutes. He had no idea what he'd say to her. He wanted her to come and live with him and Piper, but he knew he couldn't ask her to give up this life.

He didn't want to ask her to give it up. Her job was danger-ous, but he knew there might be other kids Piper's age who would need Justine's protection. Need her skills to save them, and he couldn't—wouldn't—ask her to give that up.

He just needed to know that she was his. He needed some confirmation that together, the two of them were going to be a couple.

He went down the steps and followed the garden path to-ward the fountain in the center. She was sitting on a stone bench on one side.

"What are you doing here, Nigel?"

"I came to see you."

She looked small and fragile in this garden, not at all like the warrior he knew her to be.

"Why?"

"You left the hospital without saying good-bye."

She stood up, wrapping her arms around her waist. "I'm sorry about that. You and Piper were sleeping when I left."

He made his way slowly around the fountain to her side. He couldn't wait another second to have her in his arms. The dis-tance, the awkwardness between them, melted away as he pulled her close to him.

He kissed her hard and held her as tightly as he could. "I love you, Justine O'Neill, and I'm here to see if you will spend the rest of your life with me."

Justine hugged him so tightly that he felt her small bones through the layers of his clothing. "Sit down, Nigel. There is more you need to know about me before you ask me that question."

Justine didn't know if talking more about her past would af-fect Nigel or not. But she thought Sam had been right when he'd told her she couldn't move forward while she was hiding from her past. The girl she'd been was long gone, but the people who had been affected by that one incident were still around.

Nigel sat down on the bench she'd vacated, and Justine realized she had no idea where to start. She probably should just start at the beginning, but words weren't easy for her when she thought about her past.

"Um . . . . Sam mentioned you wanted the name of my stepfather."

"Yes, I did ask him for that. I hope you don't mind, but I needed to know, to help bring some closure to the past for you. I wanted to know the full story."

Justine paced in front of him. "Do you doubt what I said?"

"No," Nigel said, standing back up. He took her hand in his. "I wanted to make sure that I could protect you from any harm."

"That's silly, Nigel. I'm not the kind of woman who needs protecting."

"I know that, but I'm the kind of man who feels the need to take care of you. I don't know if you can understand that, but I have to do everything I can to keep you safe. The same way I do for Piper."

"You're saying I'm the same to you as your daughter?" she asked, unable to resist teasing him.

"The only way you and Piper are the same is that I love you both."

That confession gave her a little thrill. "Nigel?"

"Yes, love?"

"I love you, too." She wrapped her arms around him and rose up on her tiptoes. "My stepfather was Franklin Baron. He was Derrick's father. I don't know if Derrick blames me for his father's death. I don't believe they were close when Franklin was alive."

Nigel took a step back, and then sat down again. "Franklin Baron?"

"Yes. I had a different name back then. I left the past behind when I walked out of the juvenile center."

"Thank you for trusting me with this. I . . . I don't know how our lives will be together, but I can't just quit my job."

"I'm not asking you to. I'd like to find a way to make peace with my past . . . I don't know that it's fair to say I'll spend my life with you until I do."

"Fair enough," Nigel said. "How long do you think that will take you?"

She shrugged. "I'm not sure. I was already tired of running before I fell in love with you, but it's not right to ask you to put your life on hold while I—

"Justine, I need you in my life. I need to have the woman I've come to love by my side. My life was so one-dimensional before you."

"It wasn't. You have a real life and a real chance at being normal, Nigel. With me in your life, you won't have that. I'm never going to be one of those corporate wives. I can't fit into that mold."

"I'm not asking you to."

She shook her head. "I can't do that to you. You need a woman who will be home every night, and who can complete your family with Piper."

"Justine?"

"Yes?"

"I'm not home every night, and Piper travels with me. We have made our own normal, and I'm asking you to be brave enough to come with me and be a part of our family."

She didn't want to say no, but she was very afraid of committing her life to Nigel. Of saying she'd be a part of a family. She hadn't been a part of a real family since her father had died, and the next family she'd had had been so fractured . . .

"I'm scared."

"I am, too. I have no idea how this is going to work. I only know I need you in my life."

He drew her close, holding her in his arms. She heard the French doors open, and then Piper's singsong voice calling for Nigel.

"Over here, Pip," he said.

She came over to where they stood, and when Justine would have pulled away, Nigel's grip on her kept her by his side.

"Are you going to be part of our family?" Piper asked Justine.

"I'm not sure. What do you think?" Justine wasn't leaving the most important decision in her life to an nine-year-old child, but she couldn't be a part of Nigel's life without the consent of his daughter. She wouldn't do to Piper what her mother had done to both her and Millie.

"I wish you would be part of our family," Piper said.

Justine smiled down at the little girl, and Nigel opened his arm, beckoning his daughter to join them. She ran and jumped in her father's arms, and Nigel lifted her up. Piper wrapped one arm around Justine, drawing them together as a family.

Justine took a deep breath and let it out. This was it, she thought. The change she had been looking for wasn't going to be found in running away and starting a new life. It had been found in looking inward and accepting herself. Now she could start a new life with the man she loved, and his daughter.

Get in the holiday spirit with TO ALL A GOOD NIGHT, a sexy anthology from Donna Kauffman, Jill Shalvis, and HelenKay Dimon. Check out Donna's story, "Unleashed" . . .

An hour later, she was quite thankful for the addendum maps, as she'd be hopelessly lost without them. Actually, even with them she'd gotten herself somewhat turned around, out at the end of the west wing—at least she was pretty sure it was west. Even the dogs had given up on the adventure and trotted off after some time, to God knew where. She was sure they'd find her when they got hungry or wanted to go out, so she wasn't too concerned about that. But she was getting hungry herself and she had no idea how to get back to the kitchen, much less the garage, or the rooms she'd been assigned to stay in.

She was stumbling down a dark corridor, unable to find the hall light switch, when a very deep male voice said, "If you're a burglar, then might I direct your attention downstairs to the formal dining room? The silver tea set alone would keep you in much better stealth gear for at least the next decade. At the very least, you'd be able to afford a flashlight."

Emma let out a strangled yelp as her heart leapt straight to her throat, then she froze in the darkness. Except for the animals, she was supposed to be completely alone. Not so much as a valet or sous chef was to be on the premises for the next twelve days. Of course, the notebook did say that Cicero had a lengthy and amazing vocabulary. But he was at least two floors away. And she doubted he knew how to use the house speaker system. Armed with the notebook and not much else, Emma decided offense was the best defense. "Please state who you are and how you got in here. Security has already been alerted, so you'd best—"

Rich male laughter cut her off. "You must be the sitter."

"Which must make you the burglar, then," she shot back, nerves getting the better of her.

More laughter. Which, despite being sexy as all hell, did little to calm her down. Because, though she'd been joking, the idea that she'd been on the job for less than two hours and had already allowed a thief into the house was just a perverse enough thing that would actually happen to her.

The large shadow moved closer and she was deep into the fight-or-flight debate when a soft click sounded and the hallway was illuminated with a series of crystal wall sconces. Emma's first glance at her unexpected guest did little to balance her equilibrium.

Whoever he was, he beat her five-foot-nine height by a good half foot, which made the fight thing rather moot. Flight probably wasn't going to get her very far, either. He had the kind of broad shoulders, tapered waist, and well-built legs her defensive-line-coach dad would recruit in a blink, and charming rascal dimples topped by twinkling blue eyes her Irish mother would swoon over as she served him beef stew and biscuits.

Emma, on the other hand, had absolutely no idea what to do with him.

There's nothing better than a hero who's HOT AS HELL. Keep an eye out for HelenKay Dimon's latest, coming next month from Brava. . . .

Only one thing—one person—hovered in her mind. Noah. Desire whipped through her with an intensity that threatened to knock her backward. The craving swamped all of her good sense, beat down her firm resolve to keep Noah at a distance and replaced it with a burning need.

She blamed the lust simmering inside her on the shot of adrenaline she experienced this evening. The mix of shock at seeing a dead body and terror over everything that came after.

No matter what the cause, all she wanted to do was jump on top of Noah and wipe the memory of the terrible night out of her mind. Which was why she entered the room and then stood as far away from him as the small space would allow.

She had hoped the passing minutes would kill the Noah need bouncing around her belly. But the longer she watched him turn his hands over and stare at the invisible spot on the floor, the more she wanted him focused on her.

Breaking off their engagement destroyed a part of her. The aftermath was even worse. Cleaning Noah out of her head and her heart proved impossible. As long as he lingered in there, what could one, or two, lovemaking sessions hurt? They both needed the release. They were there, adults and still attracted.

And making a move served another purpose. Hard for Noah to quick fire questions at her when he was under her.

"Are you done hiding?" His husky voice ripped to the very heart of her.

"I'm standing right here."

"Then are you ready to talk about Henderson?"

Oh, she was ready for something. "No."

He sighed. "Of course not."

"I'm done talking about Henderson."

Noah glanced up at her with a blank expression. "Because you can't come up with a believable lie?"

"Because I don't want to talk."

This was going to happen. Her. Him. Them. Bed. She missed the feel of him, his touch and kiss. Her blood surged through her at the thought of him running his hands all over her again.

"I want to help you," he said.

"Good." Because that is exactly what she had in mind. Him helping her out of this dress and into the bed.

"You have to know that I don't care what you did or didn't do."

She believed him on that score. He did not pass judgment. Did not insist that everyone live by his code. He took people as they were. Now it was time for him to just plain take her.

She closed the curtain. "That's very accommodating of you."

"To figure out the best plan of attack, you have to level with me." His dark eyes flashed with determination. So serious and worried.

She could see his confusion in the wrinkles around his eyes. The controlled anger in the way he balled his hands into fists.

"I have a better idea."

His eyes narrowed. "That's what I'm afraid of."

"Oh, I think you'll like this one."

"Hard to imagine how that's possible."

"Trust me." She walked over and stopped when her knees touched his.

The position forced him to lean back and gave her the superior power she wanted. Having him vulnerable to his needs and her wants. Hovering over him until he had to look up to see her face. Perfect.

"Lexy?"

"We could talk and talk, but you know what, Noah?"

"Uh, no."

She crouched down with her palms on his knees until they were face to face. "I'd rather sit on your lap."

"*What*?"

"Kiss you all over."

She felt him tense. Saw a flush creep over his skin. Watched every bone in his body snap to attention.

He blinked a few times. "You're saying—"

"Feel you slide inside me."

He grabbed the bedspread behind him with both hands. "I sure as hell hope you're talking about sex."

"Hot, sweaty, fantastic sex."

Heat replaced the confusion in his eyes. "With me?"

The idea of letting another man touch her left her cold. "Only you."